INTO THE

RAVINE

RICHARD SCRIMGER

TUNDRA BOOKS

To my readers

❖

Published in Canada by Tundra Books,
75 Sherbourne Street, Toronto, Ontario M5A 2P9

Published in the United States by Tundra Books of Northern New York,
P.O. Box 1030, Plattsburgh, New York 12901

Library of Congress Control Number: 2007920590

Library and Archives Canada Cataloguing in Publication

Scrimger, Richard
    Into the ravine / Richard Scrimger.

ISBN 978-0-88776-822-4

    I. Title.

PS8587.C745I58 2007 jC813'.54 C2007-900222-6

We acknowledge the financial support of the Government of Canada
through the Book Publishing Industry Development Program (BPIDP)
and that of the Government of Ontario through the Ontario Media
Development Corporation's Ontario Book Initiative. We further
acknowledge the support of the Canada Council for the Arts and the
Ontario Arts Council for our publishing program.

Design: Jennifer Lum

ONTARIO ARTS COUNCIL
CONSEIL DES ARTS DE L'ONTARIO

Printed and bound in Canada

1 2 3 4 5 6   12 11 10 09 08 07

Down the hill and through the trees
Though what you find there may not please,
Down the stream and through the wood
To say good-bye to childhood.

– not Stephen Sondheim, *Into the Woods*

Well, did you evah?
What a swell party this is!

– Cole Porter, *DuBarry Was a Lady*

. . . mostly a true book, with some stretchers, as I said before.
– Mark Twain, *The Adventures of Huckleberry Finn*

THE IDEA

NOT **A PREFACE**

I hate prefaces – never read them. It's like the author is dipping one toe in the pool, worrying about how cold the water is. Me, I'm a jumper. Sometimes I don't even bother to take off all my clothes. Drives my mom crazy. "OMIGOD, Jules!" she yelled at my dad's company barbecue last week. "What are you doing in the deep end with the polka-dot shirt you begged Baba to get you for your birthday, that you haven't written a thank-you note for yet even though I keep asking you, and now the colors will run like your sister's wool hat. Do you remember when her face turned blue and your father looked up the symptoms and found methahemoglobinemia, and then got thrown out of the hospital for yelling at the doctor? Do you remember, Jules?"

Mom gets carried away, so far away, in fact, that sometimes she forgets where she was going. My friend Chris says I take after her. My point is that prefaces are cryptic and confusing. They always seem to take place thousands of miles from where the story starts, with characters you never see again. In a word, they stink. Check this one out:

Midday sun shone on the Aeropuerto Internacional El Dorado in Bogotá. At the window by the departure gate stood Señor E, a man with a long, wrinkled face and a sharp nose like the front of a sailing ship. He watched the baggage handlers closely, paying particular attention to a large plastic carrying crate marked *Fragil*. So much depended on that one piece of baggage. The idea had seemed foolproof when young Bunky had suggested it, but now Señor E was beginning to have his doubts. So many things to worry about: the professor, the *teniente* from Muzo, even something as natural as the process of reptile digestion. Señor E recalled a quotation from the classics and smiled bitterly. "Fate is not an eagle – it creeps like a rat."

See what I mean? Do you have any idea what is going on or who these people are? Will you remember them later? Of course not. I'm confused myself, and I wrote it. The secret to enjoying a book with a preface is to skip the preface and move on to the story. Meet the hero and the mission, find the best friend who tells jokes. And look out for bad guys and falling rocks.

So, hello. My name is Jules. You know a little bit about me and my crazy family. You've heard me mention my friend Chris, who I guess is the real hero of this story. You haven't met Cory yet, but you will soon.

Yup, I'd say we're good to go here.

On to Chapter One.

The hideous monster crawled through the rubble, dripping with its own slime and the blood of my friends. I steadied my weapon. I'd only get one chance. The monster was close enough to sense my body heat. It pivoted toward me, its head the size of a small car, its nutcracker jaws shaped in a startling caricature of a smile. When the jaws parted, I'd have a fraction of a second before the squirming, flesh-sucking tentacles spilled out. Steady, Jules, I told myself. I took a deep breath, and . . .

Sorry.

That's still not the story. I got distracted.

Let me explain. It's August in Scarborough, the sprawling suburb I call home. For me, August is a time of burnt front lawns, humming power lines, melting pavements, panting dogs, and no friends (Chris is at his cottage and Cory at some kind of camp). But Scarborough has a split personality. A paved wasteland of strip malls, gang violence, and cookie-cutter bungalows, it is crisscrossed throughout by a network of startlingly beautiful ravines. Our subdivision is called Highland Heights because the houses back onto the top of a ravine, with the Highland Creek at the bottom. And the creek is lovely. It's the strangest thing – you cough your way off a bus beside six lanes of snorting, snarling traffic, but if you walk two blocks and slide down a hill you can dip your feet in a plashy pool, surrounded by woods, weeds, water, and peace.

Beauty in the midst of strife – that's what poetry is, isn't it? Or am I thinking of basketball? Anyway, mornings after breakfast, my dad picks up a briefcase, my mom picks up a laundry basket, and I take my notebook and come down to Dun Killin to write.

Dun Killin is our sanctuary, Chris's and Cory's and mine, a shallow cave in the ravine at the bottom of our backyards. You can't see the entrance unless you're looking right at it, and sometimes not even then. We found it by accident a few years ago, mining for gold, and decided to move in right away. (The mining was going very badly, unless you counted a vein of *Good Housekeeping* magazines.) It's civilized, for a cave, with a rocky ceiling and dry floor, and tall enough for Cory and me to stand up in (Chris has to hunch a bit). There's lots of light when the sun is going down because the cave faces west. Its full name is Dun Killin Zombies – Cory thought of it, even made a poster that we hung on a root sticking out of the back wall. Zombies and drawing are about the only things Cory can concentrate on for any length of time.

Right now I'm sitting on one of our chair logs, using our table stone as my writing desk. A couple of minutes ago I noticed an ant – huge black one, long as my thumb – crawling across the table. I got to thinking about it, and I got distracted, and my pen moved without me paying attention. My point is that the hideous monster has *nothing* to do with the story. Nothing at all. Sorry to mislead you.

I'll flick the ant off the table . . . all the way off the table . . . Okay, now I got it . . . and begin Chapter One again. Let's see. It all started . . .

Well, when?

It all started when we rounded the first bend of the creek, so that the deeply overhanging trees stood between us and the familiar stretch of shore, and we could no longer see the waving sunburnt limbs of our parents, or hear their laughter, and we three boys knew that we were beginning a long and important journey on our own, alone in the vast, quiet emptiness of nature – quiet, that is, except for the hum of the expressway in the distance, and alone except for the kid in the Bart Simpson T-shirt picking his nose on the far bank.

No, it started before then. It all started when we first got the idea for the raft.

It all started with the storm.

CHAPTER ONE – *Finally*

We were in Dun Killin, trying to figure out what to do. It was only the first week of summer holidays, but we were already bored. Chris wanted us to try something out of his current favorite book, *The Outdoor Survival Guide*. "Rappelling," he said. He showed me a picture of people falling down a cliff face.

"Give me that." I flipped through the book. Every page seemed to involve something dangerous. Eating poisonous mushrooms, breaking a leg, bleeding profusely. Yeck.

"Or" – I handed back the book – "we could go up to my place and make s'mores. I saw the recipe on the back of the cereal box this morning. S'mores are easy. I don't know if we have any marshmallows at home, but we can always walk to the store and get some."

Chris frowned. "*Marshmallows.*"

"Oh, go rappel yourself," I said.

He pushed me, and I pushed him back, and we were about to have a play fight, which I would have lost, when Cory suggested invading Italy.

"That's the boot one, right?" he said. "We could invade like anything! Start at the toe and pour in like . . . toasters!"

Toe to toasters. That's Cory for you. Chris caught my eye.

"Italy," he said.

We usually ended up agreeing about Cory. But Chris is such a literal guy, I can't help teasing him now and then. "Come on, man. One key to an invasion is the prize. And Italy has great ice cream. Remember the gelato your mom brought back from downtown? We'd be far from home, but we could live off the land. We might even be able to toast stuff."

"Huh?"

"If we pour in like toasters, I mean. Right, Cory?"

Cory, who is small and round and hard all over, like a rubber ball, grabbed one of the zombie-killing clubs we keep in the cave. "Or Pickering," he said. "We could invade Pickering. That'd be cool too."

He ran outside and began hitting trees with the club.

"Well," I said to Chris, "Pickering is closer than Italy." It's the suburb beside Scarborough. "Another key to an invasion is getting there. You attack next door, then keep going. That's how all the empires are built."

"Idiot," Chris muttered.

The hot afternoon had turned suddenly strangely cool, and the dark clouds were bent like brackets (yes, this kind). We followed Cory to the storm drain, the only open area of the ravine. There's a beach of small stones sloping down to the creek from the drainpipe. Chris and I started looking for flat ones to skip. Cory clambered up to hit the pipe with his zombie club.

"What do the undead heat their houses with?" he asked. He has a million of these jokes. Some of them are okay – most aren't.

"I don't know," I called.

"*Zomb-oil!*" He laughed loudly, hitting away at the pipe.

"Have you ever seen clouds do that?" I asked Chris. "Bend across the sky, I mean?"

He shook his head.

"Do you get it? That's oil, for zombies."

"Yes, Cory, we get it." My stone skipped across the riffled surface of the water. Chris watched carefully. "That's four," I said. "Not bad, huh?"

Cory beat a tattoo on the drainpipe while he stared at the sky. He had the look he gets sometimes when he's trying to figure out a color.

Chris skipped his stone with a wicked sidearm delivery, twisting his lanky body like a pretzel. He's a great baseball pitcher. Good quarterback too.

We counted together. "Seven," said Chris and punched me in the arm.

A while ago I drew a line down a sheet of paper and made a list of all the things Chris can do better than me, and all the things I can do better than him. It was kind of funny. On his side of the paper were all the sports and games. Chris is a natural athlete, fast, strong, graceful. He gets good marks too – better than me, for the most part. And he's so popular. There's a group of girls who wave at him when he strides by. He'll wave back, or nod, and the girls will all fan themselves and swoon. If I'm with him, I'll say hello, but it comes out as a soprano-baritone – "He-LLO" – and they giggle. (Not that they have a great sense of humor. They never giggle when I tell a joke.)

On my side of the paper was *Eat hot dogs*. That was the only thing I could think of that I did better than Chris. At Nancy's birthday party last year I ate seven, and Chris stopped after four. (I don't always eat that much, but I was trying to impress Nancy. I think it worked too. She went, Ew.)

When I showed the list to Chris, he tilted his head to one side. "You talk more than me," he said.

We were standing under an archway in his garden. He jumped up and hung from it, swinging gently. "In fact, you talk more than anyone, Jules." He started doing pull-ups. He's always exercising, testing himself against an unseen adversary. Or maybe he's just passing the time.

"Okay," I said. "But do I talk *better* than you?"

He stopped halfway down, elbows bent outward, biceps bunched up like baseballs. No effort showed in his face while he considered the question.

"More." He gave me a tucked-in smile and let himself down.

"Ha ha ha," I said.

He did another couple of pull-ups and dropped, landing on the balls of his feet. He took a step forward and launched himself into a perfect cartwheel.

I sighed. I couldn't do a cartwheel to save my immortal soul. One more thing to add to the list on Chris's side.

Cory was lying on his back in a pile of pebbles, looking up at the sky. He began waving his arms and legs back and forth, the way you make snow angels. I guess you can make angels out of anything.

"Green," he said. "Asparagus-green sky."

Chris and I shrugged at each other. Cory moved onto our street back in grade four, and we've hung out together ever since. He's awfully funny in his strange way. You never know what he's going to say. Teachers get upset because he disrupts the class, calling out randomly, "What are we *doing* here?" or "Who else smells cheese?" It's hard not to laugh.

He's special, but not the way the teachers use the word, meaning slow. He really is special. Maybe he's a beat behind in math and reading, but he's a *great* artist. His spaceships or zombies look like you'd see on TV, and he can do cartoons too. And he knows every color there is. Cory is just, well, Cory. Teachers don't ask him to take off his red cap anymore. That's Cory, they say. Chris and I don't hang out with him to be nice, or because our moms said we had to. We like him. And he gives us something to share. I sometimes wonder if we'd be as good friends if Cory wasn't there.

One day last fall when we had a supply teacher, Cory smuggled a squirt gun into class. Got her in the back of the neck, then put the gun away. She went ballistic. When she turned away, he got her again. He got her four times before she spotted him. "Stand up!" she screamed, her face working overtime. She was a big old lady, wore a lot of makeup. And angry – whew! I swear there was steam coming off the top of her head, though that may have been from the water. "Give me that squirt gun!"

But it's no good getting angry at Cory. He put the gun down the front of his pants. "Come and get it!" he said. The class burst out laughing, like thirty balloons popping at once.

When the teacher sent Cory to the principal's office, he pointed an accusing finger at her and bellowed at the top of his lungs, "You just hate me because I'm black!"

Pin-dropping time, then the class laughed harder than before. I don't know how funny it would have been if Cory actually was black, or brown, or beige, but he's real pale, and we all thought the comment was funny as hell.

(Just to finish this part off, if you're wondering. The principal, who is white, suspended Cory for three days. I worried that maybe I was being racist, laughing at his joke. Chris didn't think so, but I was still worried so I asked our regular teacher. Mrs. Ottley, who is black, laughed her head off – but then, she knows Cory.)

A bolt of lightning split the sky. A wall of wind knocked Chris and me flat on our backs beside Cory. There was another bolt of lightning and a near-instantaneous, near-deafening crack of thunder.

Lying on my bed of pebbles, I wondered if I was seeing things. I climbed with difficulty onto my knees, grabbed Chris's arm and pointed. I didn't even try to speak over the noise of the wind.

He was staring at it too. From the center of the swirling, circling, clearly *greenish* sky – yes, Cory, sorry for doubting you – a piece of dark cloud began to descend.

A tornado.

Our part of the world doesn't get tornadoes. I had only seen them on TV. This one didn't look like *The Wizard of Oz*, I tell you. Not a real funnel shape. It was too narrow at the top. The fat, wobbly spinning piece of cloud drooped, like a . . . well, to me it looked like the sky was clenched over a toilet bowl, taking a dump. The rolling thunder only reinforced the image.

Cory stood in the middle of the path, facing the wind. Good thing the red ball cap he wears all the time is too small for him. A normal-fitting cap would have blown off. His expression was exalted. "It must be a hundred and forty-seven miles an hour!" he shrieked.

The cloud drooped lower and lower, and began to narrow at the bottom and widen at the top. Now it looked like a funnel.

Chris and I grabbed Cory and ran him up the path to the top of the ravine as the rain began. We raced all the way to my place. I was so scared I didn't notice I was puffing and panting.

We usually end up at my place. Chris is an only child. His mom and dad work downtown, an hour away, and they don't want us playing at their house unsupervised. And Cory's house is crazy. There's about a dozen small kids running around, smearing one another with mud and mayonnaise and getting stuck under things. (Cory has brothers and sisters, and his mom runs a daycare.) Anyway, my place is where we hang out. With my sister, Julie (yeah, I know – Jules and Julie – go figure parents), moved out of the house, Mom tends to pour all her caring and worrying on me. That makes her sound like a pot full of sauce, which is actually a pretty good description. She's round and full, and she likes to stand with her hands on her hips like pot handles. She can be hot too – boiling hot. I'm happy to share her with Chris and Cory – there's plenty for us all.

"OMIGOD, Jules!" she cried when we tumbled through the back door. "Where have you been? I looked everywhere for you, I was so worried! Did you know there's a tornado warning? A tornado in Scarborough, who'd have thought it! Chris, your mother phoned from work, you should call her back now! Cory, Cory, how did your hands and face get so dirty? Your mother and the babies are fine, by the way, when I was there looking for Jules, they were all on the floor eating cookies. OMIGOD, there goes a lilac bush, blowing right across the lawn, your father will be so upset, he planted the lilacs so he wouldn't have to look at Mr. Freshanti sunbathing next door. Did you hear the siren? Did you? We should all go to the basement, that's what they said on the weather channel. Chris, bring the phone downstairs. Come on, hurry!"

So we went downstairs to the rec room, and Chris called his mom to say he was all right, and my mom brought down sandwiches and cocoa, and made Cory wash his hands and face and call home and leave a message, and we watched TV and ate while the lights flickered and the storm raged around us.

I was nearest the phone when it rang. "Hello?" I said, my voice cracking in the middle of the word.

"Jules? You, Jules?"

"Oh, hi, Baba." No mistaking that accent. She's the only grandmother I've ever known, and of course I love her, but she's not always easy to understand. She came from the old country back about the time of the Crusades, but she sounds like she just got off the boat.

"Happy birthday, Jules."

My birthday wasn't for another month, but what the heck.

"Thanks, Baba."

"What you want for present?"

"Uh . . . sure, Baba. A present."

"No no. *What* present?"

"Oh." What did I want? "I don't know, Baba." Why do old people put you on the spot like this? "Uh, a shirt?" I said.

"Good. Good." She said something in Macedonian. "Shirt. Now you ask how are you, Jules?"

"I'm fine, Baba."

"No no, you ask me."

Macedonia is way over on the other side of Italy, one of the little countries that used to be something else. As I understand it, everything is perfect there, so I don't know why anyone would leave, but they did, thousands and thousands of them, including all my grandparents.

There are so many Macedonians here in Scarborough that Baba never had to learn English. Talking to her can be a trying experience. Trying to understand what she means. Trying to get off the phone.

"Jules? You ask how I am doing."

"How are you doing, Baba?"

"Fine, Jules – except I am topless!"

She cackled. That's my baba. Always with the jokes. Gosh, I hoped this was one of them. I couldn't help shuddering, though.

"You want to talk to Mom?"

"Eh?"

My mom was on her feet, reaching for the phone. A little sigh escaped her, like steam from under a pot lid. She has more energy than anyone I know, but Baba can wear her out. "Sho preish," she said – Macedonian for how's it going?

Chris was at the window. "Storm's over," he said.

"Let's go outside and see what's been wrecked," said Cory.

Mom was leaning forward, her eyebrows together, talking into the phone. I don't speak Macedonian except for "Hello," "Thank you," and "I want some milk," but I could follow this conversation exactly. "OMIGOD, Mama!" she was saying. "What happened?"

Is it only **CHAPTER 2**? –
I've been reading for hours!

My backyard looked like it had been in a fight. The wind was dying, the sun peeping out, but the storm had left its mark. Leaves and branches littered the grass. A lawn chair – one of Cory's – lay on its side in the middle of our flower bed. The tree my parents had planted this spring was tilted at a forty-five-degree angle, and the lilac bushes were gone, so that you could see the deck where Mr. Freshanti – the stomach that walks like a man – sunbathes in a Speedo. (*Yeck!*)

Cory's house is on the other side. Carrying his lawn chair, we pushed through the gap in the hedge. His back-yard always looked beat up, so the effects of the storm weren't as obvious. A girl was making mud pies. Skinny thing with long hair in dreadlocks – not one of Cory's sisters. The back door was open, and his mom was calling.

"Dora, honey, close the door, the bugs are getting in."

"Okay." She didn't move.

"Dora, honey, please."

"Okay."

Finally I went to close the door myself, stopping in the doorway to say hello to Cory's mom. She was in an armchair in the living room, nursing a baby. There always seems to be a new baby around Cory's place, but I have never seen any men. I've taken health education, so I know this isn't right. Cory has never mentioned his dad.

"Why, hello, Jules! Don't you look nice in your striped shirt."

Cory's mom always has a smile and a kind word. And she's so *relaxed*. If my mom is a boiling pot, Cory's barely simmers. Or maybe she's not on the stove at all.

"Is Cory with you?" she asked, burping the baby and settling it on her other side. I guess she hadn't checked her messages. A diapered boy ran around her in endless circles. Another one was watching TV.

"Yes, ma'am," I said.

"I figured he was. That was quite a storm, eh?"

Somewhere in the house, something fell with a heavy thump, and a kid started to cry.

"In here, honey." Cory's mom didn't get up.

Dora wandered over, wiping her muddy hands on her shirt. I let her in and closed the door.

"Let's get going," said Cory from behind me.

The ravine is steep, and that afternoon it was mostly mud underfoot. Good thing there were lots of ferns and small trees on both sides of the path to hold on to. We slithered to the bottom, turned right, and made for the three tall poplars that grew in front of Dun Killin.

And they weren't anymore. Not tall, that is, or growing. Now they were three *long* poplars. Plucked out like rotten teeth, they lay on the ground with their roots exposed. The earth all round was plowed and torn up into dark, smelly mounds.

"The tornado did this," I said. "It must have touched down right here."

Cory wasn't interested. "What do you call an undead Canadian?" he asked.

Everything about the ravine was clearer after the storm. The smell of the turned earth and green moss, the trickle of the creek, the call of a blue jay a few trees away, and the buzz of a distant chainsaw.

Chris put his arms around the nearest tree and tried to lift it, testing himself.

"A *zomb-eh*," said Cory. "Get it?"

An idea began to form in my head. Usually my ideas arrive already made. There's a knock on the door of my brain, and someone from Federal Express is there with an idea. But sometimes I make them myself. It's like I have a workshop in the basement of my brain, and I mess around down there, putting things together, gluing, hammering, and I . . . come up with something. That's what was happening now.

"Hey, Chris," I said. "Where's that rappelling book?"

He frowned. A handsome guy lifting a tree. He looked sort of like a superhero and sort of ridiculous. "*The Outdoor Survival Handbook*," he said with dignity.

"Yeah. Show it to me."

Chris put down the tree and reached into one of his oversized pockets. He wore hiking shorts, with loops and snaps and spring-loaded clasps for carrying tools.

He handed me the guide and watched me flip through it. "That's not where the rappelling is."

"I know." The page I remembered was toward the back. I found it and spread it open to read. There was my idea, in perfect working order.

"*That's* what we'll do, guys," I said, handing him the open book.

The section was called "Raft Construction." It told you how to take logs and turn them into a serious raft. It told you what tools you needed, and what to do with them. It was a set of instructions, like the kind that come with the Ulppslie desk from IKEA, only more straightforward. (My dad got stuck on Step 4D – assembling the hutch superstructure – quietly put down his screwdriver, walked out of the house, and drove to Montreal, where he stayed for two days, sulking. My mom and sister and I never got 4D, but we figured out the rest of the desk. I still use it.)

"Forget rappelling, boys," I said. "Put the Italian invasion on hold. Let's make a raft out of these tree trunks and float it down the creek."

There was a moment of appreciative silence.

"You mean like they did in *Doc Zombie IV, Escape from Tomorrow*?" said Cory. "When they rode those giant logs down the Amazon, and the zombies all drowned?"

"Yeah, like that," I said.

"How far down you want to go?" Chris asked quietly.

"All the way," I said. "All the way to the lake."

Scarborough is enormous. It takes a half-hour to drive across it into the city, and at least that long to drive from the zoo at the top end (it's like there's a border guard of wild animals) down to the lake. Our subdivision is about in the middle, so we were looking at a serious trip here. An all-day venture.

Chris clapped me on the back.

"Good one," he said.

"You know, I could murder a root beer," said Cory.

An hour later we were poring over a map. The next day we were collecting tools from our three garages. A week after that we were packing the communal knapsack (we each contributed essentials to be shared among us: cell phone, juice boxes and oatmeal cookies from me; chewy bars, more juice boxes, rope, and an emergency kit from Chris; ketchup packets from Cory, "In case we get fries and need more ketchup") and heading down to the launch area.

I'm skipping stuff here, but you don't need a minute-by-minute description, do you? In a movie they'd do it as a montage. Working music for the scenes of us carrying the saws and rope down to the ravine, humorous music for the scenes when Cory sawed the tip off his shoe and I lashed my own hand to one of the logs, and then triumphal music as we raised the raft on its end and let it go with a splash into the creek. Water flew into the air like a crystal fountain, the raft floated, and we three gave one another a slightly silly high-five.

And then it was Saturday morning, quiet and hazy hot, with a ten percent chance of showers and a hint of something chemical in the air. We waved good-bye to Chris's and my parents and my baba and Cory's mom and baby brother, who had come down to the creek to see us off, and Chris took the long pole we'd cut to steer with and pushed the raft into the gentle current, and we drifted around the overhanging trees of the first bend and realized that we were almost alone in the vastness of nature.

The kid in the Bart Simpson T-shirt finished picking his nose. He stared at us from the far bank. "Cool raft," he said. He was about our age, with a freckled grin and a missing front tooth. His presence was a good omen, I felt. As if the spirit of boyhood adventure had come down to wish us luck.

"Your name wouldn't be Huckleberry, would it?" I called.

The kid shook his head. "Dakota."

"Oh, well. Not your fault."

"What are you talking about?" asked Cory.

"Nothing."

Chris got it. He smiled and punched me in the shoulder. I punched him back. Cory laughed. Boys on a raft in the sunshine, nothing more innocuous. Who'd have guessed that by nightfall we'd be in police custody?

THE HOLE

CHAPTER 3 – *Pretty much on schedule*

Y ou're probably wondering what Baba was doing at my place. Funny thing. Our ravine wasn't the only place to get hit by a tornado. At almost the same time, another funnel cloud was touching down in the west end of the city, near Baba's retirement home. Took the roof right off it, leaving her – you got it – topless. They had to close the whole place. She moved in with us. She's still there, sleeping in the rec room. Dad has never put in so many hours of overtime.

Highland Creek goes . . . well, it goes from left to right as you face it from Dun Killin. On the map it goes from top to bottom. We were rafting down the bottom five inches or so, at two miles to the inch. *The Outdoor Survival Handbook* says you should figure on moving about two miles an hour in open country, so the whole trip should take about five hours. The plan was for us to phone when we got to the park at the bottom of the river, and Chris's dad would come by with a trailer to carry us and the raft back home.

"It's almost nine," I said. "So we should reach the lake by, what? Two o'clock? Three o'clock? What do you think, Chris?"

He pushed us carefully forward, letting the current guide us. He looked like a gondolier with the pole in his hand, ropy muscles sliding up and down his forearms. I like Chris a lot, but there are times I can't help envying him.

"Depends," he said.

I was staring at the map. We were heading south-ish. The first big cross street we'd hit was Lawrence. After that, Elgin. Then St. Clair. Then . . .

"Depends? On what?"

"On how fast we go."

He gazed ahead, angling the raft away from the rocks.

"We might hit a waterfall." Cory was up in the bow, peering ahead. "That'd slow us down."

"What waterfall?" I said. "This is a creek, Cory. The water's up to your knees most of the time. The water can only fall a foot or so."

"Or savage tribes. They could be watching us from those trees. They'd attack us and take us captive. We've got to be ready."

He was thinking of his zombie movie again. The raft heeled slightly as I moved forward and put my hand on his shoulder. "It looks jungly here because the trees come down to the water's edge, and there's no one around except us, and it's quiet and kind of spooky. But looks can be deceiving, Cory. On top of those hills up there are bungalows. Nice, safe, modern, boring homes with picket fences and garages and 2.4 children inside. We might meet some of these kids as we drift along, but I don't think they'll be any more savage than we are."

Heat hung around us like smoke. I could feel my skin warming up. Sweat popped out of my forearm like fat bursting from a grilled sausage. I splashed water on myself, felt better. The sun caught the ripples behind us, turning the green water into links of silver chain.

I took a turn poling. Chris sat down cross-legged and reached into the knapsack for a drink. Cory stayed up front, on the alert for zombies.

I tried to imitate Chris, lifting and lowering the pole in one smooth motion. It was hard work. A pole is not a steering wheel. I'd push forward, the current would take us a bit to one side, and the front of the raft would start to turn. Then I'd push at an angle to correct the turn and the current would send us toward the side. The creek was as wide as a side street, the raft about as wide as a car, and I kept running into the curbs.

Cory used his zombie-killing stick as a fender. "You bumped again, Jules," he said. "That's nine times now. Four on the left side and five on the right."

"Thanks for counting," I said. Sweat stung my eyes, and my hands slipped on the pole. I was trying not to be irritated, and failing.

"Chris didn't bump at all."

"I'm pretending this is pinball," I said.

Chris smiled.

The crunch as we hit gravelly bottom sounded like a stegosaurus biting into a cookie. Cory teetered and sat down. Chris slid into the water, pushed the raft into the current, and leaped back aboard, all in one motion. He moved so fast that it was a wonder he got wet.

Floating round the next bend, I felt like I was watching one of those makeover shows where the rough-looking, shaggy girl turns into a babe. Good-bye wilderness, hello park. The steep, heavily wooded hillside flattened out and tamed down. There was a soccer field on our left, a picnic area on the right, and a rounded wooden bridge linking them. There was a parking lot filled with vans and SUVs. A couple of women in ball caps and short shorts ran past, awfully quickly. A man ran toward them, smiling hard as they met and then dropping his jaw to gasp for air when he was past them. An old lady was throwing a stick for her little dog to fetch.

A safe and happy scene. You could use it to sell real estate, or insurance, or laundry soap. In a way it was an improvement on the ravine – there was a breeze blowing, for one thing, which made it more comfortable. But it wasn't as much *fun*.

It reminded me of shopping for clothes with my mom. When I was small we'd go into the city, to a warehouse in the heart of the garment district. The owner smoked cigars and yelled at the customers. It was kind of scary to shop there, especially since there were no change rooms and I had to take off my pants in front of all the other ladies and their kids. But it was exciting too. I liked the noise and the dust, and Mr. Fleisher (that was the owner's name) always gave me a chewy sucker on my way out and said something to make Mom laugh. He retired a few years ago, and the place is condos now. Mom buys my clothes at Sears or Wal-Mart, and there are change rooms and it's cleaner and more convenient, but, well . . . it's not the same.

I brought the pole over to the side of the raft and pushed, trying to direct us between the two middle what-do-you-call-thems that held up the bridge.

What do you call them, anyway? Hang on a sec while I look it up.

(Pillar. *A supporting structure at the connecting spans of a bridge*. See pier.)

Okay, I was heading us between the pillars. It looked like a tight fit.

"Watch out!" cried the old lady in a clear voice. The stick landed at my feet.

Cory screamed, "Grenade!" and jumped into a surprisingly deep part of the creek. His red cap, with him inside it, sank beneath the surface. I laughed. A few nights before, we'd seen a movie where the British commandos destroy the German sub by dropping a grenade down the hatch.

Unfortunately, when I laughed the pole slipped and we turned sideways and banged into the bridge thingie – pillar, I mean.

A black, ratlike dog with floppy ears stood on the bank and barked rhythmically. *Yap yap yap*. Pause. *Yap yap yap*. He splash-swam across the creek and clambered on board, taking two tries to get up, with a *yap yap yap* in between.

"Satan!" cried the old lady with her hands to her mouth. "Oh, Satan, dear, are you all right?"

Not something you hear very often. I did a kind of double take. Chris's face went blank.

The current held us sideways on to the bridge. We weren't going anywhere. The dog pounced on the stick and picked it up in his mouth.

"Here, Satan!" the lady called. "Come back to Mommy! There's a good doggie! Come back and Mommy will give you a treat. Here, boy!"

The old lady held out her hands. She didn't look like Satan's mommy. She wore white slacks and a blue jacket, like a sailor captain. Her white hair was tied back in a tight bun. Her eyes sparkled.

The dog poised himself to jump but didn't.

"Oh, Satan, you bad dog!" The lady looked at me apologetically. "I hate to trouble you boys, but . . . could one of you carry Satan back here? Sometimes he gets nervous."

Chris was in the water, turning the raft around so that it would fit between the bridge pillars. "You want to take the dog?" I asked him.

He shook his head without looking up from his task.

"You're already wet," I said.

Chris didn't answer.

Satan was wagging his skinny rat tail. The lady smiled at me. "Sure, ma'am, I'll take him." I tried to pull the stick out of his mouth, but he wouldn't let go. So I picked him up, stick and all, and stepped into the creek. The water swirled around my bare shins. (We were all in shorts, of course. Chris had his Joe Camper ones with the zippers and hidden pockets. Cory and I wore surfer shorts that were really bathing suits.) The dog squirmed under my hands. "Here we go, Satan," I said.

Chris let out his breath in a long hiss.

The dog's fur was smooth and matte black. I could feel muscles close to the skin. His whole frame shook in time to his growls.

"Is his name really Satan?" I called.

"All creatures answer to Satan," she said with her sweet smile.

I carried the wet dog to the bank, where he dropped the stick, shook himself, and trotted off to pee on a bush. The woman thanked me. Taking in our raft and knapsack, she asked if we were on a long journey.

"All the way to the lake," I told her. "There's a park at the bottom of this creek."

"I know it well," she said. "I live just outside the park gates. Satan and I walk to the little museum every night, rain or shine. He likes to chase sticks and dig, don't you, boy? Quite intrepid of you three to be rafting all the way down there. It's wonderful to be *doing* something, isn't it? On a Saturday in the summer, every child should be doing something!"

I was fascinated by her voice. It reminded me of a milkshake: soft, sweet, liquid.

"When I was a girl, my friend Mary Lee and I played in the ravine behind her house. Tarzan, Robin Hood – all kinds of games. Mary Lee was a minister's daughter, and we played African missionaries for a while, though the only heathen we ever converted were the Siamese twins from down the street who were sweet on me." Her eyes softened, and her cheeks bloomed with color as she looked backward through the years.

I didn't know why she was telling me this, but I like stories.

"Go on," I said.

"Billy and Raymond weren't Siamese, of course. That's what we called conjoined twins back then. They used to compete for my attention. Billy wrote poems and gave them to me behind Raymond's back. Raymond embraced Jesus first, wading into the river so I could baptize him, and nearly drowning his brother in the process." She chuckled. "That was the Humber River, on the other side of town. I haven't been back in a long time."

I heard Chris calling Cory's name. He had the raft spun around, facing downstream between the bridge pillars.

"Isn't Cory out of the water yet?" I said.

Chris shook his head.

The lady called her dog back. "Come on, boy. Regan's soccer game is starting." She clipped him into a leash and led him across the wooden bridge.

I looked up and down the bank, but I couldn't see Cory.

"Enjoy your adventures, young man," called the old lady. "Keep your heart open at all times. And your eyes too, of course."

I waved at her, somewhat preoccupied, and stepped off the bank.

"Cory!" I called. No answer. I stepped forward and went down like a stone. I had no idea there were places like this in the creek bed. I felt like I'd stepped into a manhole.

I didn't panic. I'm a good swimmer. I kicked my feet, struggling toward the surface. Then I realized that my glasses were gone.

This was serious. Wearing or not wearing glasses is not a question of vanity with me. I'm as blind as a mole without them. Forget about seeing the blackboard, I can't see my dinner plate. Without glasses, I'd starve.

I tried to find them now. Opening my eyes didn't help much – all I saw was a green blur. I waved my arms wildly, hoping to knock against the glasses. I waved lower and lower.

Got them!

No, I missed. I touched them, though. They were near my left hand, and sinking. I dived, kicking my feet, waving my hands in front of my face, lower, lower, lower.

How deep was this hole? I felt like I was in a nightmare elevator, endlessly descending. Darker, colder, deeper. I waved my arms more and more frantically, hoping to make contact, knowing that every passing second made contact less likely.

Something grabbed my hand and held on.

CHAPTER 4 – *But you'll be too mesmerized by the suspense to notice*

*H*oly crap!

My first thought was that I'd been caught in the reeds. I'd heard about that happening, guys twisting themselves around underwater until they were all wrapped up in reeds and couldn't get out.

I tried to pull my hand free, but I couldn't. The grip on my hand shifted. Now it was grabbing my arm. I was trapped by some underwater creature. I pulled as hard as I could, bringing the creature right up to my face. And I saw it was Cory.

Bubbles everywhere. He was still breathing.

Together, we pulled for the surface.

I guess the sun was shining when we got there, and the sky was blue and the grass was green and the parking lots were filling up with soccer moms and dads. I didn't see any of it.

"Jules!" Worry in Chris's voice.

I held Cory's head above water. He was gulping air. He'd been under a long time.

"Stay back, Chris!" I shouted. "It's deep here."

I swam a stroke or two, put out my foot, and touched creek bottom. The relief was overwhelming. I took a step, dragging Cory after me.

Something poked me in the chest. "Ouch! What is that? What are you doing?"

"It's the pole," said Chris. "Grab it."

"I can't see it. I know it's in front of me, but I can't see it. You know how bad my eyes are, Chris."

"But it's right in front of you."

"I still can't see it."

Two strides later the water was knee-deep. We stumbled over to the raft and sat down.

If you wear glasses, you'll know how I felt without them: powerless, unhappy, strangely calm. There was nothing I could do about anything. I had no idea what was going on. The world was too far away from me.

"What happened?" asked Chris.

I looked in his direction, but all I saw was a Chris-like fuzz. "Somewhere out there" – I took a huge breath – "the creek is about twenty feet deep. There's a sinkhole or something." Another breath. "Cory and I both ended up in it."

"Black," said Cory very calmly. He was hardly breathing heavily at all. He'd been down much longer than me. One of these days I'm going to have to get myself in better shape. "Black black black." He could have been talking about the mud at the bottom of the creek bed, or the hopeless drowning feeling, or the color of his true love's hair. Speaking of black, though:

"Where's that dog?" I asked. "Satan. And the old lady?"

I saw a dim, dark outline shimmer. I guess Chris was shrugging.

"You know, you're going to have to talk more," I said.

I heard him snort. He does that when he's amused but doesn't want to show it.

"Black dog gets the sugar – white dog gets the blame," said Cory.

Thank you, Cory. Very helpful.

"You want to look?"

"For my glasses? Not down there."

Chris made a Chris-shaped gesture.

"Oh, yeah. Glasses." Cory held something out. "Here, Jules."

He opened my right hand for me and put my glasses on my palm.

The world returned to me. A bit out of focus, but I wasn't complaining.

"Thanks, Cory. Where did you find these?"

"My pocket."

He turned to show me. The back pocket of his flower-pattern surfer shorts was ripped and hung open. I guess my glasses caught on the flap of cloth and dropped in.

"Ha ha. Jules looks funny with his glasses crooked."

They sat at a slight angle on my nose. No matter. I could see pretty well if I concentrated. In a while, I'd get used to it and wouldn't notice.

Hadn't the old lady said something about keeping my eyes open?

"Funny, huh?" said Cory. "Your glasses end up in my pocket? I wasn't trying to catch them either. It was too dark to see. Remember how dark it was?"

"Shut up," I said.

I didn't want to think about it. I hunted through Chris's emergency kit for an elastic band and looped it around the earpieces of my glasses to hold them to my head. And if you think I should have thought of that earlier, well, you shut up too.

I wrung out my T-shirt and put it back on. "Now" – with my feet wide apart, hands on hips – "let's get out of here."

We edged the raft between the pillars. Chris and I crouched as we passed under the bridge. Cory lay on his back and appeared to go to sleep. His T-shirt dripped onto the bumpy logs. He wore running shoes without socks, and I noticed a patch of mud on the inside of his ankle. It stood out, dark and shiny, against his white skin.

The creek bank was thronged with bug-eating birds, zipping around after the gnats and water skeeters and mosquitoes and flies. I poled carefully, looking straight ahead, waiting for my wide-open eyes to adjust to a skewed reality.

CHAPTER 5 – *Already?*
That last one was pretty short

For an hour we poled past backyards that sloped gently down to the creek. I didn't realize Scarborough had such nice houses. They were better than ours in every way: wider, taller, cleaner. The trees were leafier, the flower beds brighter, the lawns greener, the tree houses and swing sets more elaborate. There were swimming pools, and tennis courts, and pergolas. (I think I mean that. I'll look it up.) We stared like tourists.

"That burnt sienna place looks like a castle," said Cory. "See, it has a tower and everything."

"Don't point," I said. "And anyway, the place next to it is just as big."

"It'd be cool to live in a tower," said Cory.

"Yeah, your windows would be rounded."

"And you could drop stuff on people down below."

I laughed. Cory was right – it would be cool to live in a tower. But . . . but . . . as we drifted along, I couldn't help thinking that viewing all these mansions in a row made them seem *less* impressive, not more. Lined up like cans of salmon, they seemed to lose their value. There was a sameness to them and a seemingly infinite supply. Scarcity is important. Do you like cashews? I do. If I'm imagining the perfect recreational moment, it would have to include cashews. But how many? Let's see . . .

Jules Karapoloff sprawls in a comfortable chair with his feet up. Playing on the giant TV in front of him is a brand-new episode of his favorite show, with a new episode of his other favorite show coming up next. On the table beside him is a stack of comic books, adventure stories, video games, DVDs, and a can of frosty-cold root beer. He has a handful of jumbo salted cashews, and tosses them into his mouth . . .

Pretty good. Pretty darn good. But this is paradise we're imagining here. There's more than a handful of your favorite food in paradise.

Jules Karapoloff, thirteen, sits in a comfy chair, holding a bowl of cashews . . .

Still not enough.

A big bowl of cashews . . .

Nope.

Jules reaches into a bucket full of jumbo salted cashews, which he just dragged up from the cashew-filled Dumpster on the front lawn . . .

Do you see what I mean? My baba has a saying: "If one egg is good, two eggs are better." But ten eggs aren't better than two. Enough is as good as a feast, but too much is too much. Staring up at the rows of monster houses, I found myself underwhelmed.

(By the way, I did mean pergolas.)

This part of the creek bottom was made of fine sand. We ran aground with a sound like bread being buttered.

"Off!" called Chris, who was poling.

I looked over the side and felt funny.

I thought, What if it isn't as shallow as it looked? What if I go down and down?

Cory said, "Wahoo!" and jumped, sinking over his shoes into the mud.

"Aren't you afraid?" I asked him.

"Afraid of what?"

"Well, what if there's another hole here, like there was by the bridge? What if it's deep?"

Cory shrugged. His shirt and shorts and cap were still pretty wet from the last time he jumped, but he didn't care. "If it's deep, it's deep."

Hard to scare Cory. I like to think I'm a chicken because I'm more imaginative than he is.

"Off!" called Chris.

And so, with my heart beating on my ribs like a grumpy neighbour on an apartment wall, I stepped into shin-deep guck.

Nothing happened to me. The breeze blew through the grass, the reeds rustled, the birds called, and we sat in the middle of the creek with the water rippling gently past us. I walked forward, pushing the raft, until the channel got deep enough for Cory and me to climb back on.

Cory was picking at his ankle. The black patch of mud was still there.

"What's this, Jules?" he asked. "It won't come off."

I looked more closely. It wasn't mud after all. The thumb-sized blob stood out from his skin like a giant blood blister.

He tried to pull it off, but it was stuck on.

"Leech," said Chris calmly.

A leech! A bloodsucking worm. My *second* thought was that Cory must have scraped his foot along the bottom of the deep part of the creek. Who knew what creatures lurked down that manhole to hell? The leech must have been working away at him ever since.

No leeches on me. That was my first thought. I'd even taken off my sand shoes to check my feet.

"How do I get it off me?"

"Stop pulling at it," I told him. "Leeches have tiny little teeth. They'll tear your skin and flesh away if you pull them off. You have to use salt. Sprinkle salt on a leech, and it'll curl up and die. Right, Chris?"

He nodded, tall and strong and competent, with the pole in his hands and the sun behind him making a halo. He could have been an ancient warrior, a Viking or something, if Vikings wore shorts.

"Unfortunately, Cory, we don't have any salt," I said.

Oatmeal cookies, yes. Ketchup, certainly. But no salt.

"Fire works too," said Chris.

"Oh, yeah. Remember that movie? The hero used his cigarette."

"Great!" said Cory.

"Why is it great?" I said. "We don't have any cigarettes."

If only I smoked. The tobacco lobbies should spend more time talking about the practical benefits of smoking. *Cigarettes are cool – and useful for removing bloodsucking parasites!*

"Fire!" Cory's eyes gleamed. He loves everything

about fires. He used to carry his chair through the halls. He'd stand on it to pull a fire alarm and keep moving. He always looked like he was going somewhere. It took them the longest time to work out who was doing it.

"I have a cigarette lighter," he said. "I stole it from my mom."

The raft went aground again. It was really shallow here. There were stones set up like a path across the creek.

Chris put down the pole. Water rippled gently against the sides of the raft. We weren't going anywhere.

"We'll do it now," he said.

Cory had the lighter out. Flicked it on and off.

I turned away.

"Hello, mister!" A child's voice, English accent, calling from the near bank.

I was startled. "You talking to me?"

She was maybe eight, with long dark hair and a beach ball held in front of her like a shield. Beside her was a boy, younger, with his mouth closed and his eyes wide open.

"Is that your boat, mister? Are you allowed to play in the creek?"

I'd never been called mister before. I nodded.

"We're not. Our daddy says creeks are dangerous, doesn't he, Edwin?"

The boy nodded vigorously so that his whole body moved back and forth, like a reed in the wind.

"Jules," said Chris.

"Where Daddy is, they have piranha fish in the creeks. They can strip you to the bone in ten minutes, Daddy says. Right, Edwin?"

The boy's mouth opened and a single word came out.

"Bonesaw," he said. He had a strange voice for a little kid – raspy, like it hurt him to talk. His accent wasn't as strong as his sister's.

"Yes, Bonesaw too."

They wore rich-kid clothes, everything clean and matching, but I couldn't help thinking that here they were on the edge of the dangerous creek and no Daddy in sight. Not even a babysitter. The big house with the red roof and the black iron shutters was a long way away.

"Jules!" said Chris.

I turned around. My two friends looked like they were frozen in the middle of a wrestling match. Cory lay on his back with his left leg in the air. Chris was on his knees, twisting Cory's ankle, leech side down.

Cory held the lighter up to me.

"Do it, Jules," he said. "Kill the leech!"

"I don't want to," I said. "I might burn you."

"If you don't do it, I will," said Cory. "And I'll burn myself for sure. I can't even see where to hold the lighter."

"*You* take it," I said to Chris.

He shook his head. He had both hands wrapped securely around the raised foot.

"It has to be you, Jules," he said.

"I –"

"Hurry."

He was the leader of our group. I did what he said.

I took the lighter and knelt beside him, bringing my head to leech level. I brought the lighter up, spun the flint wheel against my thumb.

This close up, Cory's leg was a blur through my bent glasses. "Hang on," I said, closing my eyes tight.

We were doing a stupid thing. Stupid and wrong. With my eyes closed I saw it clear as crystal. What kind of choice was this – either I burned my friend or else I stood aside and let him burn himself. Why did these have to be the only options?

I opened my eyes wide, blinked twice. Cory's ankle swam into clearer focus. Up close the leech was a spongy black mass, all bumps and ridges.

"What's going on, mister?" called the girl.

I flicked the lighter, to test it. A finger of flame shot out. I imagined the flame hitting Cory's skin. He probably wouldn't cry out, because he's too . . . well, too weird, but the fire would eat at him. I imagined it crisping his ankle, blackening it like a spare rib on the barbecue.

I couldn't do it.

I turned to the two kids on the bank. "Do you guys live there?" I nodded at the house with the red roof.

The boy, Edwin, nodded vigorously. The girl said, "Yes."

"Do you have any salt in the house?" I asked.

"Salt?" she said, pronouncing it carefully: *solt*. She frowned, maybe wondering if we were talking about two different things. "As in salt and pepper?"

"Yes. Do you have any?"

"Well, certainly. Do you want to borrow some?"

I sighed with relief, stood up, and put the lighter in my pocket.

INTERRUPTION Number 1 – Life

It's hard to be taken seriously when you tell a lot of jokes, but every now and then I get a deeper thought. Give me a moment here, and then I'll go back to my strange and mostly goofy story.

The way I see it, you start out in life playing in a field, running around with your arms spread in the wind, pretending to be a horse or an airplane or something. And the air is fresh and sweet-smelling, and it's always sunny and warm, and the grass is soft when you fall down dizzy from running. That's childhood. Then you start to learn stuff – counting, tying your shoes, eating with a fork, like that. One day you look around and notice that there's a gate in your field. A way out. Maybe you want to go through the gate and maybe you don't, but the field is getting crowded and the gate is always open, and so you go through it. Now you're on a road. You look back, but the gate is closed behind you.

Pretty soon the road starts to climb. It rains, and gets colder, but you keep going. It gets steeper, even dangerous, but you press on, because there's nowhere else to go. The road leads to the city at the top of the mountain, and that's adulthood. Every now and then you come to an easy stretch of road, where the sun breaks out and there's a picnic or a ball game, and you can take it easy, but you can be sure that you'll start climbing again soon, even steeper than before. And all the time you're climbing, you're learning things. You learn how big your heart is, and how small your hand. You learn to look away. You learn that you can't put the rain back in the sky. I don't know what else you learn, because I'm still climbing and I'm nowhere near the top. (My big sister, for instance, is not interested in Halloween anymore. I'll take all the free candy I can get.)

Anyway, as you walk along, you come to signposts. These are the moments that show how far you've come. Do you remember your first lie? No, me neither. But do you remember the first big lie? And getting caught. And saying, "Oh crap" to yourself. That's a signpost. Remember the first time you looked down and saw hair? Actual hair on your lip, or your leg, or under your arm, or – well, I remember vividly because it wasn't that long ago. I showed my forearm to Nancy, sitting next to me in geography class. She said, "Ew."

Speaking of which, do you remember hearing your first real swear word? I was in the mall with my dad, and these big kids were talking outside the shoe store, and they said the f-word. I must have heard it on TV, because I knew it, but I'd never heard it in real life before, and my jaw clattered onto the floor. Dad stopped, put his hands on his hips. They were three or four kids, all bigger than him. "Nice talk," he said, moving in close to the biggest of them. "Nice talk for my son to hear. Jules, aren't these cool guys, with their muscles and tattoos? Don't you want to be like them? Don't you want to learn to swear? We'll ask this boy to say the word again. Could you say it again, please?" I wanted to die, but the funny thing is, the big kids did too. They shuffled off. Back home, hanging up our coats, I told the word to Mom, who slapped my dad across the face. And I saw that, just as the boys were afraid of him, he was afraid of her.

And now here was another signpost. No one had ever called me mister before the little girl on the creek bank did. I must be getting closer to the top of the mountain.

When I look down the road behind me, I can see how far I've come. My memory of childhood is fading. Every now and then, when I'm feeling low, I think it'd be neat to run one more time with my arms spread wide, smelling the sweet grass. But once you leave the field, you never go back.

THE GANG

Let's see, we've had five . . .
so this would be **CHAPTER 6**

The girl's name was Daisy – Daisy Aherne. Edwin was her little brother. We followed them up the lush back lawn to the basement door, and then upstairs to a main-floor kitchen bigger than my whole house. I stared at the bed-sized countertops, the gleaming silver fridge, the hanging rack of copper pots and pans. It might have been a Pottery Barn showroom except for the three bowls by the sink, with a familiar dark residue in them.

Edwin, who had seen his kitchen before, shrugged and trotted back downstairs. Daisy found a salt shaker on one of the tables.

For Cory, the chrome silver stove was a magnet. He moved toward it without a word and started twisting dials. Blue flame rolled out of the burners, circling them like a halo. Cory chuckled. The gas hissed.

What was he going to do next? Maybe he hadn't thought that far. Cory wasn't a chess player, planning several moves ahead. He was more a scratch-it-when-it-itches guy.

"What the hell?" I cried. "Cory, you can't just walk into someone's house and turn things on! What if they had a burglar alarm, and you turned *that* on, and the police came and shot you? And you bled so much you needed a transfusion, only the blood was tainted, and you ended up with . . ."

While I was talking, Chris moved like lightning, pulling Cory away from the stove, turning off the element. Cory opened his mouth. Chris put out his hand and covered it.

"No," he said.

". . . hepatitis?" I said.

Daisy was looking confused. "Sorry," I told her. "Cory's like that sometimes." She gave me an unconvinced half smile.

There was a bathroom next to the kitchen. Sink and toilet and wallpaper in the same light blue. We crowded inside and held Cory's ankle over the toilet and sprinkled salt on his leech. It twisted up and fell off, and that was that.

Daisy put down the lid of the toilet seat.

Have you finished? said a deep voice from the back of the tank.

The room was small. The voice echoed alarmingly. I stepped back, bumping into Chris. Cory leaped a foot in the air.

"Was that the toilet?" I whispered.

Daisy nodded. "Yes, mister. It's automatic."

Have you finished? asked the toilet again. *If you have finished, say, "Finished."*

"Finished," said Daisy.

Thank you. And the toilet flushed.

Cory yelped like a spaniel.

"The toilet talked!" he said. "The Dodger-blue toilet talked and flushed."

Chris and I exchanged glances.

"Does it say anything else?" I asked Daisy.

"No."

I tried to imagine a conversation with a toilet. *How ya doing? Say, I'm thinking of a number between one and two . . .*

"Potty mouth," Chris murmured.

"I know. I know. There are too many jokes to make here," I said.

Cory was jumping up and down. "Hello, toilet," he said. "Hello. It's me, Cory. What's your name, toilet?"

Chris and I led him out of the bathroom, still talking.

We traveled along a quiet hall, with carpet that tickled my ankles, down a different set of stairs than the ones we came up, and through a rec room in the basement to get to the back door. Edwin was there, sitting in a fuzzy kid chair watching rhinos on TV. I couldn't get over this great big house, and no one around except two small children. Saturday mornings at my house there was Mom cooking breakfast, Dad yelling at the newspaper, my sister calling to complain about her university courses or her roommates or her job, my friends ringing the doorbell or barging in to steal my extra pieces of toast. I won't say it was a symphony, but it was sure lively. In this place, the only voices these two kids heard belonged to the TV and the toilet.

"Where are your mom and dad?" I asked Daisy.

"Daddy's in South America." She pointed to a

framed map on the wall. "He's a professor. And Mommy's sleeping. Don't worry about Edwin and me. We're okay. I made Count Chocula for our breakfast."

Ah, yes. The familiar dark residue.

"Is anyone looking after you?"

"Bonesaw," said Edwin in his queer, raspy voice. He pointed at a door with a KEEP OUT sign.

"Don't be silly, Edwin. Bonesaw isn't watching us. Philip is. He's our big brother, mister," she explained.

I wondered if Bonesaw was a code word or a person. "Is that Bonesaw's room?" I asked Edwin.

He nodded solemnly.

"Don't go in," Daisy said. "No one's allowed in Bonesaw's room."

Edwin pointed at the TV screen. "Philip's going to *see* the rhinos," he said.

Chris jerked his head at the door. He was right – it was time to be getting back.

"Thanks again," I said to Daisy. "Thanks a lot for the salt."

"No problem, mister." But the shadow of trouble swam briefly in her eyes, there and then gone, like a big fish in murky water.

Chris saw them first. Without a word he took off, racing down the gently sloping back lawn toward the creek. Cory leaped after him, slower and more noisily.

"Hey!" he shouted.

Now I saw them: three strangers, messing with our raft. Two of them stood on rocks at opposite ends of the raft, kicking it, making it bounce up and down. The third stayed on the bank with his hands in his pockets. They all wore baseball jackets.

I ran, pumping my arms, concentrating on my breathing. *In*, two three four. *Out*, two three four. Cory pulled away from me, still shouting. Chris ran right up to the kid on the bank and stood there, with his chest out and fists clenched. Chris is a scary sight when he's mad, but the other kid wasn't backing down at all.

The other two left the raft alone and came over to stand beside their guy.

Oh, no, I thought.

In, two three. *Gasp*, two three four. By the time I arrived at the water's edge, I was puffing like a grand-dad over a birthday cake. Yes, I really must try to get in shape.

"Get away from our raft!" said Cory. "It's our raft! Ours!"

We were all on the bank now, faced off against one another in two lines. I was the only one breathing heavily.

"So," said one kid. "This is *your* raft."

He talked like Daisy, in an English accent. This had to be brother Philip. Some babysitter he was – letting his little sister invite strangers into the house while he wandered around with his friends. He wore a thick neckchain and had a sharp face like a fox. He was smaller than his friends but clearly the leader, the little dog at the head of the pack.

I considered us all, as my breathing got less ragged and my heart went back to doing the speed limit. They were a bit older than us – high-school age. Not too much bigger but a lot tougher. (The jackets helped, and the nose ring one of them wore.) Somehow we were just three guys hanging out, and they were a gang.

"Yeah," said Cory. "Our raft."

"Well, when we take it away from you, it'll be *our* raft."

"Oh, yeah?" said Cory.

"Yeah."

"Yeah?" said Cory.

"Yeah."

"Hey," said Cory, deviating from the script. He cocked his head. "Anyone else hear that noise?" He walked carefully away from us, peering downward into the reeds. "There it is. A frog!" He bent down.

Ah, Cory.

Philip shook his head and turned back to Chris.

"It's our creek. You lot are trespassing. Everything in our creek belongs to us. And that includes your cute little raft."

"No," said Chris.

Never one for debating, Chris.

As I think I've said before, I'm a chicken. (Yes, feel free to make all the *pawk . . . pawk* jokes you want.) I do not like the thought of danger or physical pain. I'm not even comfortable in this kind of confrontation.

Philip didn't mind it at all. He smiled broadly. And I grew even less comfortable. Partly, it was his teeth. They were too big, and too many, for his mouth. It looked like they were dumped in by the tooth fairy while she was thinking about something else. They stuck out at angles, like the teeth of a saw. His smile frightened me, but the scariness was more mental than dental. When he smiled, you saw that there was something odd inside him. Something lived behind his eyes, an animal in a cave. It came out of the cave now and sniffed the air.

"Colin," he said, snapping his fingers, "gimme my hook."

Colin was the one with the nose ring. With his heavy brows and broad shoulders, he looked like a prize bull. He reached under his jacket and took out a . . . well, a hook. A bit too short for a shepherd's crook, but about the same shape. Philip took the hook in both hands, like a baseball bat or a golf club. It didn't look like a tool anymore – it looked like a weapon. Our little confrontation was turning into a rumble.

How many gang fights have you seen on TV or in the movies? Dozens? Hundreds? This was the first I'd been part of. When I first saw a live tiger at the zoo, I thought, Yup, that's a tiger, all right. But the tiger was safe behind bars, not pointed right at me. I don't know what I'd do if I saw a tiger in my driveway. Probably what I did when I saw Philip holding his darn hook.

I babbled.

"Guys, guys, guys," I said quickly. "Let's not be getting in over our heads here, not that the water is very deep, ha ha. How about this?" I smiled. "Maybe this *is* your stretch of creek, which would make us trespassers all right, and I can see how you wouldn't want that because trespassers are scum. I hate them myself. But – and I want you to pay attention here – the way to get rid of us is to let us go on our way. You see, the sooner we leave, the sooner we won't be trespassing, and you'll have your stretch of creek to yourselves. Huh? Is that an idea or what? What do you think?"

This all came out like . . . well, it came out really fast and loose. I always babble when I'm scared. When a bumblebee is buzzing nearby, I sound like I'm selling steak knives on TV.

It was hot down here by the creek. The breeze had died down, and the morning was marching toward boiling. I wiped my arm across my brow and tried to smile winningly at Philip.

"You know, that's a great-looking chain," I said.

The links were the shape of crossed bones. Pretty cool, if you think wearing a necklace is cool.

"Geez, Jules." Chris hadn't taken a step backward.

"Come on, Chris. Don't you think he looks cool? All these guys do. And tough. I'm scared of them, and I don't mind admitting it. Aren't you scared?"

"No," said Chris.

"But they must be feeling the heat. Aren't you guys hot? It's a day to burn your mouth on, as my baba always says – she's got a lot of expressions like that – and you're wearing jackets. That is some commitment to style." I spread my hands. Philip frowned and Colin shook his head, a bull shooing flies. The third gang member – Zach, I found out later – held his jacket open like a runway model. He was taller, rangier, and had a bandana wrapped around his head.

"Anyway, here's my plan," I said. "We jump on the raft and drift downstream and get out of your hair, and you guys go back to terrorizing the neighborhood. What do you think? Does that sound fair?"

The silence stretched and stretched – a one-size-fits-all elastic waistband of a silence. Then my cell phone rang from the bottom of my knapsack. On the raft.

"That'll be for me," I said. "I was expecting a call about now. What time is it – ten thirty? Yup. The old Saturday-morning call." I walked backward, my eyes on the group, and kept talking. No one tried to stop me. No one even moved except for Cory, who was on his knees at the edge of the water, trying to catch the frog.

I climbed onto the raft, dripping. Zach the Bandana was tall, I noticed, and he carried himself well. "Hey, you look like my friend Chris." I pointed. "That guy there. See the similarity? You could be twin brothers."

He frowned, moving his head between us. "But –"

"I mean it as a compliment, man. Chris is very popular. You should see the way the girls hang on him. He has to . . . Hello?" I had the phone out now. "Yeah, hi, Mom. Right on time. Ten thirty. How are you?"

I covered the mouthpiece. "My mom is worried about us. You know how moms are, hey?" I waved at Chris and Cory. "Let's go!" Then back to the phone. "Go on, Mom. You were saying?"

Chris and Cory pushed the raft past the line of stones and into deep water. Chris got on and picked up the pole. Mom was telling me how my father had made a snack for him and me this morning, forgetting that I was gone, and then eaten both snacks himself and was feeling sick. I said, Uh huh, and, Go on, and like that. The baseball jackets were in a trance, listening to me talk on the phone. I felt like a snake charmer. As long as I kept talking, the spell would work.

"We're on our way now, Mom," I said. "We got stuck, but now we're moving again. It's a fine day to be traveling." I waved away a bunch of gnats. "I said, Fine. What's that, Mom? I can't hear you – can you hear me?"

The raft drifted slowly downstream. The baseball jackets walked along the bank beside us, glaring. I smiled at them. My plan was working. We were going to glide gradually away. We would have too, if not for Cory.

CHAPTER 7 – *Sorry to break at such an obvious dramatic moment, but that was a long chapter*

Philip stopped, the way a growling dog will stop when you've got to the edge of its property. We were close enough to hear Bandana ask if they should keep after us.

"Nah," said Philip. "Let 'em go, Zach. Let the kids run away on their raft. We don't want to wreck our party clothes. Bernadette picked these pants out for me."

Party? It occurred to me that, under the baseball jackets, these guys were well dressed. Their shirts had buttons down the front and no wrinkles.

"Anyway, I'm supposed to be babysitting my brother and sister."

And that's when Cory opened his mouth.

"Babysitting?" He stood in the middle of the raft with his hands on his hips. "Babysitting is for girls!"

Philip stiffened.

"Shut up, Cory," I said real fast. Not because he was saying something dumb about what girls do. I was used to that. But Philip wouldn't like being teased.

Cory paid no attention, of course. He was laughing like anything. "You're a girl!" He pointed at Philip. "A girl."

It didn't occur to him that there was any danger. He was not brave, like Chris. He was ignorant of fear.

"Think you're so tough, but you're really a girl!" he said. "You wear a necklace and you babysit!"

Different people react to teasing differently. I ignore it. No point in getting upset with someone who's laughing at your egg salad sandwiches. Philip ran into the creek and swung his hook at Cory, forward and back, *whoosh whoosh*. I wondered if it was some sort of ninja weapon.

Violence is something you see every day. No matter how hard they try to make them safe and fun, every school playground in the world has some big kid intimidating some little kid. But this was violence of a different order. This was attempted assault with a weapon. Despite what I'd seen since kindergarten, it was new, and scary. And directed at me!

Your first experience of a real fight is supposed to be thrilling. Mine made me want to wet my pants.

Philip missed and stumbled on the rocks underfoot.

Chris bent low to put his weight behind the pole. The raft surged forward.

Cory laughed and did a little dance.

"You even swing like a girl!" he called back.

That Cory. Despite my bowel-loosening panic, I had to smile.

The current began to pick up speed as the stream headed downhill. The banks got steeper and wilder. We were moving at a jogging pace, with the three of them racing after us over rocks and through underbrush. Putting on a last burst of speed, Philip pulled level with the raft and splashed into the creek. He got within arm's length and swung his hook again. I grabbed Cory and threw him to the deck. Philip missed, and the creek bent to the right, away from him. He stood knee-deep in the swirling water, shaking his fist. "I'll get you!" he shouted. "You wait! You'll hear from . . ."

The current carried us around the bend, and the voice faded.

"You okay, Jules?" Chris asked.

"Think so." I was sitting up, rubbing my elbow where I'd banged it against the log. I glared at Cory, but he was on his stomach, staring down at the water.

I pushed him angrily. "What were you thinking back there?" I said. "You nearly got us all in trouble."

"Jade," he decided. "It was viridian, but now it's jade green."

"Aargh." Hard to hold his interest for long. I stood up and stretched, hearing my back crack. We were still moving along fairly well. The creek was making its way downhill, and the sides of the ravine were getting higher. The lower we got, the fainter the breeze.

"What did the guy shout?" I asked Chris.

"Bonesaw." He peered back, as if expecting pursuit.

"Yeah, that's what I heard. I wonder who Bonesaw is?"

Chris shook his head.

I remembered the flash of trouble in Daisy's face. *No one goes into Bonesaw's room.*

By now the creek was cutting through steep hillsides lined with young trees, like the ravine we knew back home. On the water, the breeze had almost died away. The air felt heavy on my skin. Gnats hung in the air in clotted millions, thick as smoke. The green water rippled past us, telling a quiet bedtime story to the rocks. I yawned.

"That was pretty weird back there, huh, Chris? Like some gang movie."

"Yeah."

He frowned at me. Something on his mind.

"I'll take over, if you like," I said.

He handed the pole to me. There was only one boulder in the next stretch of water, and I missed it but not by much. Somehow, the harder I steered away, the closer the current took us. Frustrating work, poling.

Chris phoned home. I asked why he bothered. "If your folks are worried, they'll call you," I told him.

"Said I would," he said.

"But we're not in trouble now. You don't have any news to report. You're phoning for nothing."

He raised his eyebrows. "Said I would."

"I swallowed a bug," said Cory from the front of the raft, making a face. "Gimme a juice."

Chris tossed him a box with his free hand.

"Bye," he said into the phone and put it back in the knapsack. It was his third word after *Hi* and *Fine*. The conversation had taken less than fifteen seconds.

He sat cross-legged to watch me steer. I wasn't nervous in front of Chris – never had been. We both knew he was better at whatever was being done, and that took away the pressure of competition.

He shook his head. "I don't understand you, Jules."

He wasn't talking about my steering.

"You mean back there, in front of the guys with the jackets?"

He nodded.

"What's to understand? I saw we were in trouble, and I tried talking us out of it. Would have succeeded if it hadn't been for old *Babysitting is for girls*."

"Hey, babysitting *is* for girls."

"Shut up, Cory," I said. A knuckle of land stuck up in the middle of the stream. I steered us away.

"Talking?" said Chris. "You mean lying."

Was *that* what was bothering him?

"Their jackets didn't look cool. They looked stupid. You sucked up to them and you didn't mean it. That's a lie."

I shrugged. "I never thought of it that way. Yes, I guess it was a lie."

"Lying is bad."

Chris goes to church on Sunday with his mom. They get dressed up and everything. He doesn't talk about it much, but it comes out now and then. Doing something – phoning home, say – because he said he would. When we meet a homeless guy, I'll say hi, but Chris always gives him everything in his pockets. (One day outside the candy store a hobo thanked Chris and turned to me. I said I was going to use my money to buy candy and share it with Chris. "So, really," I said, pointing to the handful of change, "that's from both of us.")

Oops. I'd pushed us in the wrong direction by mistake, toward the knuckle of land instead of away. At least we weren't going fast. I got ready to crash, but at the last moment the current caught the front of the raft and took us neatly around.

"Maybe lying is bad, but what about fighting? Isn't that bad too?"

"Standing up to bullies is the right thing to do."

"But is it the only answer?"

"Fighting doesn't make you look stupid."

Ah, so that was it. Sucking up to those guys hurt his self-image. I hadn't thought about self-image – I almost never do.

"Well, gee, Chris, I'm sorry for making you look bad. I figured those guys were bigger than us, and we'd get our time clocks punched. And," I smiled, "their jackets were stupid, but they were . . . almost cool too. It wasn't a real lie. More a *sort of* lie."

"Huh. A *sort of* lie. Like when you tell your mom you'll go straight home from school and then you don't?"

"No, no. That's just me forgetting."

He sighed deeply. "Sometimes, Jules –"

"Hey, you guys!" Cory called from the front. "How do the undead clean their hockey rinks?"

Chris and I stopped arguing, shrugged.

"They use a *zomboni*. Get it?" He sucked his juice box concave.

I decided to test a theory. The next big rock we came to, I steered straight for it. Sure enough, at the last moment the current pulled us to the side. I was starting to get this steering thing.

Cory was squinting at the creek bank ahead of us on the left. "What's that?"

Chris stood up.

I couldn't see anything. The sun was right in my eyes.

"Big animal," said Cory. "Stands out, seal brown against chartreuse leaves."

"A deer?" I said.

"Wrong color. Maybe a person. Or a zombie!" Cory held the zombie-killing stick in both hands, like a baseball bat. "Powie!" he said, taking a swing and almost knocking himself down.

"Bonesaw?" asked Chris.

"No way," I said. "We've been moving too fast. And those guys are busy, remember?"

"Babysitting, ha ha!" said Cory.

"Forget about Bonesaw, Chris. We've heard the last of him, whoever he is."

I sounded so sure of myself. I remember that.

Round the next bend, or maybe the one after that, we first caught sight of the Elgin Avenue bridge. The ravine widened out and flattened at the bottom. It wasn't a V shape anymore. Now it looked like a U. Actually (while we're on letters of the alphabet) this particular section – with the bridge running across Elgin Street – looked almost exactly like a letter D lying on its side: ▢

The sun was directly behind the bridge, so I didn't really notice it until we slipped into its shadow. I'd driven over it lots of times, and never thought about it. It was a bridge – so what? I'd never seen it from below. It was a block long, supported by huge concrete pillars set way back from the water and an arch of steel girders between them.

And it was astounding.

You don't appreciate bridges when you're on them. Looking up at this one from water level, I marveled. The smooth height of the pillars, the springy bow of the arch, the combination of beauty and strength – astounding, all right.

Chris and Cory got it too. We all stared up, our mouths open wide like baby birds begging for worms.

"That thing must be a hundred and forty-seven feet high," said Cory.

(A hundred and forty-seven is his number for astounding, as in, *I give that movie a hundred and forty-seven stars* or *Wow, Chris! You hit that ball a hundred and forty-seven feet.*)

Chris nodded. "Why we came," he said. I think he meant this was why we came on the rafting trip – to see stuff like this.

"Right," I said.

Lots of graffiti around the base of the pillars – mostly gang logos, some of them done quite well. Way, way up, where the rounded top of the arch touched the underside of the bridge, were the letters MW + CH in drippy black spray paint, with a heart around them. Someone (MW, I was betting – the letters were bigger) had climbed up the crisscross bracing of a steel girder to express their love. The writing had to be ten stories in the air. I tried to imagine doing that, and my hands got so sweaty I almost dropped the pole.

Chris was keeping watch in the front. The bow, I should be calling it.

"Bikes ahead," he called.

"You mean rocks?" I asked.

"No."

Cory hurried up to check.

"Yeah, there's a bunch of bikes in the water. They're strung all along the bottom. We're going to hit them any second. Five, four, three, two, one."

We drifted on.

"Three, two, one."

Drifting.

"Zero," said Chris, and we hit them.

"Hey," said Cory. "Look at the fish!"

Fish and bicycles. Should be a joke there. We were almost under the bridge now. The air was cooler and danker. Mosquito country. I didn't notice until one of them had sucked me dry. When I slapped it, I got blood all over my arm.

The water was shallow, rocky. I never saw Cory's fish, but bicycle pieces were everywhere, flattened and twisted into fantastic shapes, like bones in a mass grave. Weeds streamed from pedals and spokes and handlebars. No way we could float the raft through here. We'd have to drag it over.

We stepped into the water, picking our way carefully, watching for loose sharp bits. Chris was on one side of the raft, Cory and I on the other. We bent our backs and hauled. The raft scraped over twisted metal. We pulled again. And again.

"I don't get it," Cory said to me in a low voice. "Who would want to ride their bike down here?"

We got hung up when a pair of handlebars caught in the lashing between two of our logs. I shuffled over to Chris's side, and he and I lifted the end of the raft. The handlebars were still attached to a rusty old bike, and we lifted the whole thing clear of the water and held on while Cory slipped underneath to yank it free. We lowered the raft back into the water. I went round to my side, and Chris and I heaved it forward again.

Stuck. "Come on, Cory!"

He was holding the bike frame at arm's length. It had a banana seat and long chopped handlebars. Green tendrils of weeds dripped like plastic streamers.

"There's a picture of my mom on a bike like this," he said. "She keeps it in her bedroom, in a frame. She's, like, really young."

He took a deep breath and threw the bike away, as hard as he could.

"Stupid Mom," he said in a harsh voice.

Suddenly it was very quiet by the old bridge, just the water and the shade and the mosquitoes, and the echoes of Cory's anger.

I suggested a snack. So we left the raft on top of the bicycle bones and went ashore with our juice boxes and the Tupperware container of oatmeal cookies. The air under the bridge smelled of concrete and water and slime – but not in a bad way. In fact, the basementy smell seemed to match the oatmeal and raisins, and whatever else Mom puts in the cookies.

We dug in.

Have you ever felt that someone was watching you? Not like those TV shows where the stalker is following the pretty girl around with a telescope while she gets undressed. I have *never* felt that. In fact, I'd be sorry for anyone following me around, hoping for an eyeful. But every now and then I get the feeling that someone is looking over my shoulder.

I had the feeling now. I flung a quick look behind me when I was reaching for a third cookie.

And I was right. There *was* someone there.

THE HOBO CANNONBALL

was so startled, I dropped the cookie.

The shape – that's all I saw, a dark shape, like a lump of rock, but with a head on top. A human shape with large and luminous eyes peering around the edge of the pillar. Now it was gone.

Should we run away or fight? The choice streaked across my mind like a shooting star, and I was on my feet before I knew it, breathing hard, muscles tensed.

"Someone's there," I whispered.

Cory leaped up, splashing over to the raft to grab his zombie-killing stick. *Run away* isn't in Cory's dictionary. Chris found a piece of broken bicycle – a front fork – and slapped it against his open palm.

I guess we weren't running away. Okay, then. I reached down blindly and grabbed my own piece of rusted bike debris. The three of us stood in a semicircle, facing the danger, armed and ready. I got a sense of primitive connection here, a hearkening back to the distant past, cave dwellers against sabertoothed cats, hunters against wolves, travelers against bandits. The atmosphere helped: musty and dim.

Chris was frowning at my hands. I looked down, realized that the bike part I had grabbed was – a pedal.

"What'll you do with that, Jules?"

"I don't know."

I gripped the flat part where you put your foot and twirled the spindle part that connects to the bike frame. Kind of like one of those New Year's Eve noisemakers, only without the noise.

"Grrr," I said threateningly.

Chris sighed. "Oh, Jules."

But before I could make a better selection, my watcher appeared from behind the pillar.

He still looked like a lump of rock with a head on top. He wore a dark brown cape that trailed down to the ground. His eyes were too big for his round, very white face.

He spoke. "Do you boys have . . ."

He swallowed, tried again.

"Do you boys have anything to . . . eat?"

And with that he pitched forward, all three-foot-six of him. Despite his wrinkled face, he was no taller than a first grader. No longer than a first grader, I should say, since he was lying down. (Wait! Didn't I use this joke already? Let me check.) Anyway, he lay on his face, with his cape twisted around him. His running shoes were scuffed and worn. He didn't move.

"Grrr!" I spun my pedal at him. Cory laughed.

I'm not proud of this next bit. I know we're supposed to help people in trouble. Geez, my mom feeds anyone who comes to the door, hungry or not. Truth is, I felt kind of scared of the guy. It was so strange of him to be wandering around the ravine in a cape. He had staring eyes (not now, he was unconscious), long, dirty fingernails, and a crust of dirt on his arms. He was smelly, and his hair was tangled and filthy. And he was so small and creepy – like a hobo doll.

I wanted to leave him there. "He's a bum," I said. "Let's get back to our trip."

Chris wanted to feed him. "He's hungry," he said. That do-the-right-thing streak coming out again.

Cory wanted to hit him with the zombie-killing stick. "Just in case," he said. We both said no, so he went off to look at graffiti.

"So what if he's hungry," I said. "It's not up to us to feed him."

Chris didn't say anything. He looked at me – specifically, my stomach, which pushed the front of my T-shirt out over my shorts. I've thought about dieting a couple of times, but as I understand it, dieting means watching what you eat and I don't want to do that. Besides, Mom keeps baking cookies and I'd hate for them to go to waste.

"What?" I said.

He didn't say anything.

"You calling me fat?" I said.

Chris shook his head.

"The world is full of hungry people. We can't feed them all. Come on." And I turned to go.

"We can feed *him*," said Chris. And he reached into the knapsack.

"Look at him. His hair's full of crawling things. You're not his mom. You're not responsible for him."

"Hey, guys!" called Cory. "Take a look at this picture!"

"Later," I called.

Chris knelt beside the small caped figure and turned him over.

"Stop it." I pulled him away. "You'll catch something. A disease or something."

"Poverty is not catching."

Deep, huh? *Poverty is not catching.* I wish I could tell you that the line affected me, changed my mind about the plight of the homeless, or at least this guy. I wish I'd responded with something equally pithy. Not true, though. I said, "Poverty shmoverty," which is not deep at all. In fact, it's kind of pointless. Like I said, I'm not proud of any of this.

(I can't find the other time I used the tall/long joke. I'm going to let it go, I think.)

The hobo woke up and ate a cookie, and then another one, and drank a juice box. He ate politely, wiping his mouth, taking one bite at a time. He smiled and thanked us over and over. His name was Ernesto. He made us introduce ourselves so he could thank us properly. He stood up and bowed to each of us. A real bow, with one hand held out at the side. It went with the cape.

He looked good, bowing. Like he'd done it before. Cory laughed.

After a while I stopped being scared of him.

He was still creepy, though. He was dirty, and he smelled, and his nails were long, and his hair seemed to move on its own if you looked at it for any length of time. I didn't like him. In fact, I wanted to scratch myself all over just watching him. He did have a nice voice, light and clear, not at all what you'd expect. He put a space around every word when he talked. Reminded me of the guy on the opera broadcasts. (*Mimi recalls happier times. Then, clasping the fur muff her friends have brought, she dies quietly in Rodolfo's arms, as the curtain falls on Act IV.* My father ends up in tears every Saturday afternoon.)

We each had another juice box and some more cookies. Ernesto said they were the best cookies he had ever tasted. I said my mom made them, and he told me I was lucky to have a mom like that.

He licked his lips.

"More?" said Chris.

"What, another cookie? I would hate to impose. I am hungry, though."

He looked at me. I sighed and offered him the open Tupperware container.

He thanked me. "You are a jewel," he said.

"Jules," I corrected him.

"Yes."

Chris smiled.

Cory asked him if he'd always been so short.

"Cory!" I said.

Ernesto smiled to show he wasn't offended. "No, my little Joker. I was once even shorter than this. In fact, *this* is as tall as I will ever be."

"So you're a –"

"STOP!"

Cory stopped.

"You were going to use the m-word," Ernesto said, speaking slowly. "That's a bad word for short people."

"You mean –"

"Don't say the word, Joker. It would be as if you called your friend here a . . . well, a word I don't use. You may call me a 'little person' if you like. Or even a dwarf. I don't mind being called a dwarf."

"Or," I said, "we could call you Ernesto."

"Yes." He grinned at me, showing yellow teeth.

"I climbed up a telephone pole once," said Cory.

I couldn't see a connection here, but Ernesto nodded seriously. "They're tall, aren't they."

"Yeah."

I wanted to ask how he came to be a hobo. I've often wondered this. No one sets out to be a bum. It's not a career choice. No one goes to the high-school guidance counselor with a plan for future bumhood. *What courses should I skip? What exams should I fail? Are there bad life choices I should be making now?* So when it happens – to a guy like Ernesto, who sounds almost normal – you have to wonder.

Cory pulled me over to the pillar to see the graffiti. "Cool, huh?" he said. "That's cobalt." He reached out to touch the shading. The drawing looked very fresh. It was a cartoon, a skull with a saw cutting into the top of it. A particular saw, short and rounded at the top, with a curved handle and a heavy blade. I'd never seen one but I knew in a flash what it was.

A bone saw.

Ernesto insisted on helping us move the raft. "I am in your debt, Captain Marvel," he said to Chris. Funny about his names for us. Cory was a Joker all right, and Chris really did act like some kind of comic-book super-hero. I don't know about me, though. I didn't feel like much of a jewel.

For a starved little guy, Ernesto was strong. When he took off his cape, you could see the muscles under his dirty T-shirt.

We had trouble lifting the raft off the hill of bike parts. While we were straining away we heard a shriek, drawn out and piercing, from far overhead. The hair on the back of my neck stood up.

Ernesto straightened up. "Oh, yes, it's Saturday," he said. "I forgot."

Out of the corner of my eye, I got a sense of some-thing falling. I turned, but by then it had hit the water, close enough to splash us.

I screamed.

I thought it was a body. I thought someone had fallen off the bridge. When it bounced, I stopped screaming.

Not a body. A bike. It landed on its tires, bounced, and fell sideways. I heard cheering from above. People were leaning over the edge of the bridge, so far up they looked like flies on the ceiling.

"Hurry, Jewel," said Ernesto. "Before the next one." He and I pulled at the raft while Chris pushed. I felt exposed. I wanted to run. It'd be safe under the bridge.

"Bombs away!" shouted Cory. He was staring up.

Falling objects seem to be alive. Watching the red racing bike twist slowly on its way down, growing larger and more distinct, I thought of it as a body, a suicide maybe, filled now with regret. It looked like it was heading right for us, but it missed us by a mile. I never could judge a fly ball. Remind me to tell you about my baseball career.

"There'll be more bicycles," said Ernesto. "They drop them off the bridge every Saturday. It's a local project. One week they dropped ten."

Cory joined us, and we hauled like mad to get the raft safely under the bridge. I heaved a huge sigh of relief.

"Thanks, Ernesto," said Chris. He looked at me.

I mumbled something.

"It is nothing, Jewel. Nothing, Captain Marvel. I am in your debt, after all."

I was trying to understand what was happening up above. "You're saying the whole neighborhood gets together to throw bikes off the bridge? Why?"

He shrugged. "The Elgin Avenue bicycle drop is a Saturday ritual. It's been going on for years. There's a parade and a cheering crowd. Sometimes the bikes are decorated, like a ritual sacrifice. Roscoe grew up around here in the 1980s, and he remembers dropping his first bike. It's a big moment in an Elgin Avenue child's life.

Of course, there isn't much for young people to do around here."

Cory stood in the middle of the stream, shouting up through cupped hands.

"Losers! Can't hit me!" He bent over and wiggled his rear end at them.

"Our Joker is not acting wisely," said Ernesto. "Elgin Avenue kids can be . . . mischievous. They might aim the next bike at him. There have been such incidents."

"Cory!" We dragged him away.

"Do the Elgin kids have anything to do with Bonesaw?" I asked.

Chris shot me a quick glance. "There's graffiti on the pillar there," I explained. "A picture."

"Picture of what?" asked Chris.

"What do you think? Picture of a bone saw."

Ernesto reached up to grip my arm. His hands were small, powerful, filthy. I shook them off. He apologized but persisted. "What do you boys know of Bonesaw?"

C hris told Ernesto about our confrontation with the baseball jackets while we collected our snack stuff and pushed the raft over to the downstream side of the bridge. Two more bikes fell behind us – one with a splash, the other with a sickening snap, like a pulled wishbone. Cheers drifted down. Tall trees leaned over the creek, obscuring the view above. No bikes came over this side.

"*You'll hear from Bonesaw?*" Ernesto nodded thoughtfully. "These boys upstream in the black jackets said that to you?"

Chris and Cory were on board. I stood knee-deep in water at the back of the raft, ready to push us off.

"And one of them carries a hook," said Ernesto. "Hmm."

"Do you know about them?" I asked.

"We all do, down here."

"Who's we?" asked Cory.

"All of us," Ernesto held out his arms.

"Dwarves?" Cory's eyebrows popped up. He ran to the front of the raft and peered ahead. "There's a dwarf army down here?"

Ernesto smiled.

"Tell us," Chris said, "what you do know."

He held out a hand to help Ernesto on the raft. The little guy laughed and leaped aboard in one smooth motion. His cape was under his arm. He was so light, he didn't make the raft dip at all.

"Can I come too?" I asked, climbing lumpily after him.

Chris frowned at me, and I stuck out my tongue.

I know, I know. Ernesto was being a nice guy, and I was being a jerk. But once you start acting a certain way, it's hard to backtrack. Being a jerk makes you feel like a jerk, which makes you act even jerkier.

Chris poled. I stood in the middle of the raft. Cory kneeled at the front, looking for zombies and dwarves. Ernesto sat cross-legged at the back.

"This is the ravine," he said at length. "Lots of people visit. They come down here looking for peace or beauty, violence or escape, but they all go back up the hill after an hour or so. Only two kinds of people make the ravine their world. Children are one kind. They come down in the morning and stay all day, season after season, catching, climbing, growing – creating worlds where they make the rules. You three know what I'm talking about. Except that you're almost too old for the ravine, aren't you? You've already left your own part – the part you know. The creek is your childhood, and you are following it to where it ends."

I listened intently. Chris's pole made hardly any noise in the water.

"The other kind of people who live in the ravine,"

said Ernesto, "are the ones like me. Vagrants. Hoboes. Traveling men. Whatever you call us. Like children, we escape from the city and make our world down here. We don't want any trouble, so we stay out of sight. And people leave us alone. At least they used to."

He swallowed.

"All this changed a few months ago, when a small gang of teenagers started visiting up and down the ravine. Normally teenagers want to be by themselves, but this gang wanted to find us and hurt us. They come from upstream and down. Their signature is on the bridges at Elgin and St. Clair Avenue, and on the hoardings outside the Rep House by the lake. They beat up Roscoe and Billy, and chased me for half an hour, throwing things. They set fire to the Preacher's shelter, with him inside it."

Chris and I exchanged that scrunched-up *yeck* face. Cory stopped dabbling his feet in the water. His eyes gleamed. "Fire!" he said.

"No," said Chris. He put his hand on Cory's shoulder. "No."

"Is Bonesaw the name of the gang?" I asked.

"I don't know, Jewel. Roscoe knows the most. He heard them talking about Bonesaw, and there's Bonesaw graffiti on the bridges down here. He saw the boys clearly while they were beating him. They wear baseball jackets, and one of them carries a hook."

I took over the steering. Ernesto moved to the front of the raft. I didn't know how long he was going to be with us, but it didn't seem to matter. He was along for the ride. "Watch out, Jewel!" he called, but it was too late.

When we hit the bank, he did a front flip off the raft – an actual flip. He tucked his legs up and somersaulted in the air, landing on the bank with his feet together, hands raised, and a smile on his face. His teeth were as yellow as corn on the cob. Cory applauded.

"Where'd you learn to do that?" he asked.

Ernesto gave his little bow. "Ah, that's a long story, Joker."

"Tell us!" cried Cory.

"You really want to hear?"

"Oh, yes. I like stories."

Ernesto looked around. Chris nodded. I didn't do anything. Inside, I nodded. I liked stories too.

CHAPTER 9 – *The broken part*

B eing a small kid in a tough city neighborhood is an unlucky combination. How small was Ernesto? When he entered high school, he was under three feet. He had to kneel to see over his desk.

Of course, the other kids picked on him. Forget about being called names. The m-word was the least of it. He lost his lunch every day. He was picked up and carried around. He was tossed like a ball. He was stuffed into lockers, driers, shopping carts, gym bags. No point in complaining – everyone thought it was funny.

The best piece of advice he got came from his sister, Theresa. She did not tell him to stand up to the bullies. Standing up to bullies doesn't do any good when you stand waist high. Theresa told her little brother to carry a book and a flashlight. It'll pass the time, she said. And so whenever he was cooped up in something, he read. Library books, mostly – they were sturdy and free.

One fine fall day, four members of the senior football team decided to let off some steam by throwing Ernesto off the roof. Each of the Bald Eagles (so named for their shaved heads and eagle tattoos) grabbed an arm or leg, stood on the edge of the roof, and swung him back and forth. Ernesto begged them to put him down, but they ignored him. They thought it'd be funny if they could throw the dwarf over the school fence and into the swimming pool in the apartment building next to the school.

Cory laughed at this. I couldn't. The little guy flying through the air and landing in the swimming pool is kind of funny. But the Eagles were being awfully mean.

They drew him back one more time and then launched him into space.

Ernesto's eyes went all cloudy as he described falling gently through the warm spring afternoon. I thought I was flying, he said. I was weak from hunger – missed my lunch again – and then it seemed as though I didn't land!

Of course they didn't throw him near far enough. He went almost straight down and landed on the foam high-jump pit in the middle of gym class. As he shot back up into the air, he found himself turning a somersault. When he landed on his feet, the gym class applauded. When the teacher gave the Eagles a detention, they vowed revenge.

Ernesto coughed. "Sorry, boys. I am not used to talking so long," he said.

"Have some orange juice," I said. "Cuts the phlegm."

I sounded like my mom.

Chris got him a juice box. He bowed his head in thanks and sipped.

"I don't understand why they vowed revenge," I said. "Revenge for what? Doesn't revenge happen after somebody's done something bad to you?"

"You could say that I got them in trouble," said Ernesto.

I blinked. "No, you couldn't."

"Well, that's how they saw it. So the next day they really mailed me."

"You mean they nailed you?"

"No, mailed."

I don't know whether to believe this. It made a good story, the way he told it. He explained how they stuffed him in a crate, stuck a label on it, and paid for him to be shipped to Bridgewater, New Jersey. He didn't dare cry out while the Eagles were carrying him, and afterward it was too late.

"You never saw a scareder fellow than the clerk at the Bridgewater Post Office," Ernesto said. "He nearly had a heart attack when he opened the crate. 'You're supposed to be a poodle,' he said."

This I could laugh at. Cory was almost sick he was laughing so hard.

When Ernesto climbed out of the crate clutching his old library book, the first thing he saw was a full-color poster advertising the circus, which was performing in Bridgewater that evening.

Every library book Ernesto had ever read had a scene where the circus comes to town. He figured this was his chance. He ran all the way across town and presented himself to the ringmaster, who took one look at him and dragged him to the change rooms. "Put this on," he said, holding out a red-and-black skintight suit. "We haven't had anyone who could fit into this in a year."

And Ernesto, slipping easily into the suit, became The Human Bullet. (Smaller than a cannonball, but just as dangerous!) His job: to be stuffed into the muzzle of a small cannon and flung into the air. It was just what the Bald Eagles had done to him, but now he was being paid for it.

The first night was a huge success. You know how the human cannonball works, don't you? Fifty feet in the air, zero to sixty-five in three seconds, and you land in the net. Of fifty human cannonballs in the last century, thirty have died on the job – mostly by missing the net. Ernesto was unafraid. And when he found himself in the air for the second time in as many days, he did a somer-sault . . . and the crowd went wild.

"That's a great story," said Cory when Ernesto stopped speaking.

"It's not over," said Ernesto. "What happened was –"

"Rapids!" called Chris.

We made a left turn and started heading downhill. The creek chuckled along, louder than before and full of boul-ders. We bumped and spun like a dodge-em car. I was working hard to keep us front-end first. Chris and Cory were fending off all over the place.

"They're building a condo, and they've diverted the creek around the site," said Ernesto. "There's a drop up ahead."

The creek was bending east-west at this point. The sun was over the left side of the ravine, which meant that for now the right side was sun-dappled, green, and pleasant, and the left was shadowed and greeny-gray.

"How steep a drop?" I asked. I'd laughed at Cory for talking about a waterfall. Seemed I was wrong.

"How steep?" I asked again.

Shapes were emerging from the shadow side of the ravine. People shapes. Hoboes. Ernesto waved to them.

Peeking out from the foliage was a concrete tower. This would be the condo. It stood eight or ten floors high, unfinished, so that the top was jagged, like a broken tooth. A crane stood tall and silent and still in the middle of it.

We bumped hard against two rocks and held. Water rushed past us on both sides.

"Oops," I said.

"That's okay, Jewel," said Ernesto with a smile. "This is my stop. I get off here. These are my friends – some of the guys I was telling you about. Hi, Roscoe!"

"Hey . . . Ernesto," called the nearest guy in a gravelly voice.

He stood right on the bank, a wide load of a man. His arms hung straight down from massive shoulders, ending in hands the size of baked hams. His army jacket was unbuttoned. His moon face and the folds of his neck were the color of honey. They glistened with sweat.

"Who's that?" he asked, leaning forward to stare.

Ernesto was calling to the other hoboes. "Hi, Billy. Hi, Dirtbag." This to a beanpole hobo and an old guy leaning on him.

They called greetings back at him.

"Who's that?" Roscoe growled again, pointing at Chris. "I know him!"

Have I told you my baba's saying about eggs? Maybe it was true of hoboes too. If one hobo is bad, four hoboes are awful.

That's a pretty cheap joke. Actually, I was coming round to liking Ernesto. He told a good story, he could do a front flip, and he appreciated my mom's cookies. These are good qualities. His friends didn't seem very nice, though. I was apprehensive. There was a bad atmosphere here, and it had nothing to do with personal hygiene.

Chris had the same feeling. "Let's go, Jules," he said quietly.

I couldn't resist. "Don't you want to feed them?" I asked. "They might be hungry."

He glared at me, but I was already in the water, trying to swing the raft back into the current.

Cory wouldn't know apprehensive if it bit him on the arm. He stared at the beanpole hobo, trying to remember something. Finally he nodded to himself. "T-ball," he said, and strangely enough I knew what he meant. With a big, round bald head on a stick-thin body, Billy looked like a human T-ball. We'd played T-ball one summer a few years back, in an organized league. I was bad, but Cory was amazingly bad. He'd stand at the plate, hacking away at the T like a lumberjack trying to bring down a Douglas fir. If he hit it, he'd run to first base and start a fight. Once, he ran to third base. Once, he picked up the ball and stuffed it down his pants. The shortstop on the other team laughed so hard he threw up. The only reason the coach kept Cory on the team was because he came in the same carpool as Chris, and she didn't want to lose her best player.

(They talk about non-competitive leagues, but don't you believe it. I've played on fun-time teams all my life. The coach may sound as cheery as a soap commercial, but the look in her eye says, "Win, kid, or we're all going to hell.")

Ernesto was the smallest one there, of course. Yes, he was the littlest hobo. Roscoe was the biggest hobo. Billy was the tallest hobo. Dirtbag – think about a guy with that nickname in that company – was the filthiest person I've ever seen. He had a couple of gray-brown teeth and wisps of curly no-color hair sticking straight out. He wore a brown lumber jacket and one brown running shoe. His skin was flaked and granular. He looked . . . well, he looked like he was made of dirt.

Roscoe waved his giant fist at Chris. "He's . . . that guy," he growled.

"What guy?" asked Ernesto.

"The guy who beat me up. That Bonesaw guy!"

"Bonesaw!" cried Billy and Dirtbag.

The three of them waded toward us, purposefully, menacingly. They had their arms out. They looked mean and big. And, of course, dirty . . .

"Save us, Jules," said Cory.

"Yes, save us, Jules," pleaded Chris.

I looked into the eyes of my two friends, and I realized it was up to me.

Just then Ernesto made one of his leaps off the side of the raft, tucking into a somersault in midair. It was my moment. I brought the steering pole out of the water. "It's homer time!" I yelled, bringing the pole around in a beautiful flat swing. The solid hit jolted Ernesto into Roscoe and Billy. The three of them went down like bowling pins. I continued my swing around the back end of the raft, whaling into the dirtiest hobo, who fell into the creek and began to melt. Before my eyes Dirtbag literally dissolved in the water. Layer upon layer of dirt was washed away, and there was nothing left of him underneath. If not for a soggy heap of clothes and a single shoe, you'd never have known there was anyone there.

Cory stared and stared, but there was no time for wonder. I stuck my pole on the right side and heaved hard, swinging us into the current.

"What about the rapids?" said Chris.

"Who cares about rapids!" I cried. "Hang on, and I'll steer us through hell."

"Jules," was what they said, but the look in their eyes said, "My hero."

"Jules!"

Mom's voice drifts down over the ravine like smog, making my eyes water. Geez, it's embarrassing when your mom calls you in public.

I shut my notebook and hurry up the hill. She's standing in our backyard in a typical pose: hands on hips, eyes wide, mouth open.

"OMIGOD, Jules, it's dinnertime! Ribs too – your favorite. Why are you so late? We've been waiting and waiting. Your father's stomach is making the strangest noises. Baba thinks he's possessed."

And the rest of CHAPTER 9

*T*hat was yesterday. This is today, sunny and dry, typical August. Cicadas are singing their end of summer lament. It's nine fifteen by my watch, and I'm back at Dun Killin, full of spare ribs and sauce from last night and French toast and powdered sugar from this morning, and with a new pen. Looking over the last pages I wrote, I can see that I let, ahem, fantasy seep into the story.

There was no hobo baseball. No dissolving-dirt hobo either – though that was pretty cool, eh? And my friends didn't do any of that "my hero" stuff. Here's what really happened.

Cory took one look at the grim, grisly trio, marching toward the raft with their arms outstretched, and jumped to his inevitable conclusion.

"Zombies!" he cried, grabbing the killing stick and flailing it wildly. "Come and get it, you undead!"

The hoboes halted. Chris pushed Ernesto into the creek, jumped in himself to help me haul us off the rocks, and grabbed the pole from my hand. And we floated away.

(Disappointing, I know.)

I stared back at Ernesto, who was sitting in the shallows clutching his cape, the water up to his chest. His eyes met mine. His expression showed me that he was genuinely puzzled by what was going on. He lifted his hand and waved. I waved back.

Poor guy. I wondered how his story turned sour, so that he ended up leaving the circus and living under a bridge.

Funny thing about the circus. Have you ever been? Me neither. I'm not talking about the Cirque du Soleil, I mean a real circus, with animals and clowns, strong man and bearded lady, and a ringmaster in a top hat. No one younger than your grandparents has ever been to one of those. Like the steam engine, the cowboy, and the typewriter, the circus has vanished. So those kids who ran off to join the circus, where do they go now? When you think about it, a circus made a great place to run away to. All the strangeness and fun, and always moving. Like a crusade, or a pilgrimage. A traveling collection of icons.

Gee, I'm getting nostalgic here. How can I miss something I've never known?

I blame the powdered sugar. I knew I was putting on too much.

The condo rose on our right. The creek bent left around it, a sudden turn. We were in an artificial stream bed with gravel sides. Chris held the pole firmly. The water was running sharply downhill at this point and we picked up speed.

"Wahoo!" Cory sat down suddenly. I dropped to my knees. I did not want to fall in here. The water foamed around us. We bumped against the edge of the stream bed and started spinning. We raced around the condo, dropping fast, and splashed our way into a backwater full of foam.

"Can we do that again?" cried Cory.

I had to smile. He was right. It was kind of like the log ride up at Wonder Mountain.

Chris phoned home again. It was another one of those Hi-Fine-Bye conversations. He offered the phone to me, but I shook my head. Mom would call me soon enough.

"What was going on back there?" I asked him. "Did you know that hobo?"

"No."

"He said he knew you."

Chris shrugged. He poled along, his face still and closed off. He got like that when he was upset. I wondered what to do to bring him back.

"Want a cookie?" I said.

"No."

I had the Tupperware container out and was holding it out to him. He slapped it away, hard. I hung onto the container, but one of the cookies fell into the water.

Neither of us said anything.

It looked like we were in a green bowl. Rounded ravine sides covered in fresh foliage, water the color of lime Jello and almost as thick. Chris pushed us forward.

I thought about what Ernesto had said about child-hood and the ravine. I'd always thought of it as a fun place. Not quite paradise, because there were mosquitoes and garbage, but essentially safe.

It was starting to seem different now.

Do you know the Berenstain Bears books? Course you do. I didn't like the stories much, so when Dad read them to me he put on different accents to make them more interesting. He added dialogue too. (Mama Bear sounded like one of the Sopranos. *Politeness? Fugget about it!* She was tough too, hitting Brother and Sister and Papa all the time. I laughed and laughed.)

Where was I going with this? Oh yeah, in one of the books they learn about not trusting strangers, and when Sister looks at the friendly playground, she suddenly sees all sorts of evil things. (*Eh, Sistah, whatcha scared of? Go on and play, ya yutz! Whap!*)

And that's how I felt about the ravine. It had become a dangerous place. I felt like Sister Bear. We were drifting through a very pretty section now, gentle slopes with summer blooms among the scrub and trees. I couldn't enjoy it at all. I kept my eyes peeled for danger. Whenever we had to get off the raft and push, I looked over my shoulder.

I didn't trust the older couple standing in the middle of the stream. Not one bit.

DEATH

CHAPTER 10 – *And about time too*

They stood on a spit of land. Two guys. As we got nearer, I saw that they were not alone. Maybe a dozen more people lined the bank behind them. Another gang! Way too clean for hoboes, but they all looked tough. Most were in black. Several had tattoos.

"What now?" I asked Chris. I was at the front of the raft, looking out.

He frowned, shook his head.

They were kind of chanting together. It was spooky. We were too far off to hear what they were saying, but every now and then a word or two would come through.

"Still waters," I heard.

That's where we were, all right. The creek was hardly moving.

"Shadow of death," I heard, which made me gulp.

Then *"Evil,"* spoken with a sinister emphasis.

Not good. I strained to listen harder.

"In the presence of mine enemies," I heard.

That did it. I turned back to Chris. "It's some kind of cult," I whispered. "Did you hear what they're saying? It's all about death and revenge. Someone's pouring oil on their heads."

Chris frowned. "Huh?"

"It's what they said. Well, wouldn't you want revenge if someone was pouring oil on your head?"

I wondered if we could turn around, or hide somewhere and wait for the gang to go away. I didn't want to get oiled.

"They're calling up zombies," Cory muttered. "Let's attack before it's too late!"

I was thinking that Cory might have something – which only goes to show you how upset I was. We got closer, and I could hear more.

"Poor Randy," said the older guy of the couple, wearing a black leather sports jacket. He had a mustache and a small bandage on his cheek from where he'd cut himself shaving.

"This is as good a place as any," said the younger guy. He wore a black button-down shirt and tight jeans. His hair was short, showing a branchwork of tattooing on the side of his neck and around his ear.

"Let's do it!" called someone from on the bank.

Leather jacket held out a large metal jar. Everyone bowed their head.

"It *is* a cult, see?" I whispered. "Let's get out of here."

"Shh," said Chris. "You too, Cory. No noise. They've all got their eyes closed. Maybe we can float past."

He moved the pole without lifting it out of the water, guiding the raft into the middle of the stream.

I held my breath as we drifted along. The ravine was a green oven, warm enough to bake our doughy bodies while the insects worked like yeast.

The older guy with the leather jacket held the ritual jar upside down, muttering some spell or other. We drifted closer, closer. I didn't know what was supposed to happen next. A genie? An explosion?

What happened was . . . nothing. He shook the jar a couple of times and fumbled at it. Everyone had their eyes closed. We were right up to them. In another few seconds we'd be past. I held my breath. Cory stared at his zombie stick. We're going to do it, I thought. We're going to get away with this.

We ran aground right in front of them. Should have figured on it. The spit of land jutting out meant that the creek was extra shallow here.

We were less than arm's length away. It was like a game of blind man's bluff. Chris made motions with his hands, indicating that we should get off the raft and push. I nodded and slipped over the side.

The guy with the bandage and the dude with the tattoo were whispering together. Both of them still with their eyes closed.

"*Psst*," whispered the old guy. "Psst, Steven!"

"What is it, Walter?"

"I can't open the damn urn."

The water was ankle-deep. Chris and I were bent over opposite sides of the raft. He mouthed, One . . . two . . . three . . .

Walter, wrestling with the top of the urn, lost his grip and dropped it into the stream. It landed with a splash right at my feet. He swore, good and loud. And everyone opened their eyes. Steven's eyes, I couldn't help noticing, were red, as if he'd been crying.

I had the urn in my hand – must have picked it up without thinking. Seconds passed in silence, and then a strong, humorous voice from the bank called, "Why, if it isn't Tom and Huck and Jim."

People giggled. Someone said, "Shush, Terry."

The humorous voice said, "No wonder Randy liked spending time down in the ravine."

And they all started to laugh. Even Steven. Then in the middle of laughing, he started to cry.

Walter put his arm around the younger man. He was blinking hard.

The urn weighed about as much as a big book. I handed it back to Walter. He thanked me. I began to suspect what you probably know already. This wasn't a cult or a gang. They were wearing black for a different reason.

Walter cleared his throat. "Say, you boys have any tools on that raft? A pair of pliers or a screwdriver, maybe? We'd like to be able to scatter our dead friend's ashes, and we can't get the urn open."

Cory's eyes bugged right out of his head. "That's a body in there?"

I said quickly to Walter, "Don't mind him."

"But –"

"Shut *up*, Cory!"

Chris was reaching into the knapsack. "*The Outdoor Survival Handbook* says you should always carry an emergency kit," he said. "I have fish hooks and a mirror, and a knife. Here you go."

He handed a folding knife to Steven, who fumbled a couple of times trying to open it.

"Mr. Macho Outdoorsman," said Terry from the back. His friends tried to shush him, but he was unshushable. "I got a mirror in my emergency kit too."

Steven didn't know what to do with the knife. Chris and Walter both said, "Let me." There was more giggling and shushing at the back. Chris frowned like he does when he's upset. He took the blade and forced it under the lid of the urn. "See, like that," he said.

"Thanks." Steven took the knife from Chris, opened the lid further.

"Yes," said Chris. "Now you've got it."

"Quiet, everyone!" Walter said.

Silence. Steven held up the urn and cleared his throat.

"So, this is good-bye, Randy. I'll miss you at home. I know Walter and Natalie and the rest of them will miss you down at 41 Division. Hell, we'll all miss having you around. Ashes to ashes. And dust to – oh crap!"

The lid popped off suddenly and a pound or so of ashes slid out of the urn, landing in the shallows with a soft *foop*. Quite a mound there, melting and darkening in the still water.

"Now *that*," said Terry from the back, "was an anticlimax."

More shushing.

Steven sighed and shook his head. "Actually, *dust to oh crap* makes more sense than dwelling in the house of the Lord forever," he said. "I guess the ceremony is over.

This isn't Randy, anyway. We won't see him anymore."

Murmurs along the bank. I bowed my head.

"Now, let's go back to our – I mean, my place. I need a drink."

I noticed some chunks in the pile that weren't ash. Bone, I guess. I shuddered.

Walter folded up the knife and handed it back to Chris. "We really appreciate your help, boys," he said. "You live around here?"

While Chris put back the knife, I explained what we were doing.

"Hey, you've come a long way. The next big over-pass should be Highway 2, and the park isn't far after that. You'll be there for lunch."

"Try the restaurant at the Rep House," said a dark-haired woman near the front. "They do a good burger."

"No they don't. I had *the* worst meal there. Lamb, I think."

"Shut up, Terry," said a couple of voices.

I had to smile.

"The Rep House is closed," said Walter. "Building code violation. They're renovating now. You boys won't be able to eat there."

"Just as well," called Terry. "That lamb was awful."

My mom always tells me to do the polite thing. "I'm sorry to hear about your friend," I said to Steven.

"Yeah. Thanks, Huck."

Cory had been fidgeting quietly for a long time. Now he piped up.

"Are you sure you didn't come down here to call the dead back to life?" he demanded.

Walter smiled lopsidedly, shook his head. "Wish we could," he said. Steven took his hand and the two of them walked to the shore. Walter's pants dragged in the mud, but he didn't seem to mind.

We got the raft into the middle of the stream as quickly as we could. None of us wanted to hang around. Maybe Randy's spirit wasn't there, mingling with his cold, wet ashes and lumps of bone, and maybe it was. And, let's face it, ashes and lumps of bone were pretty creepy on their own.

Someone on the shore turned on a portable radio, and Randy's friends filed away, singing along with a show tune about a guy who – I think – ate his wife and divorced his lunch. Doesn't sound right to me either, but that's what I heard. There were some tears, but some laughs too. More than one of them turned around to wave at us as we drifted downstream. Chris poled along, embarrassed at the attention, but I didn't mind waving back. The funeral clothes stood out among the green and yellow of the ravine, making the mourners easy to spot as they climbed the hill, telling the world what a swell party this is.

CHAPTER 11 – *No boys allowed*

I took over the pole from Chris. He got a juice box from the knapsack, offered it around. I shook my head. Cory didn't notice. In the middle of the quietly rippling water and humming insects, Chris spoke.

"Sorry, Jules," he said. When I'm apologizing, I usually keep my eyes on the floor, but Chris looked right at me.

"You talking about the cookie you knocked in the water?"

He nodded. "And Ernesto."

With Chris, you sometimes have to dig to uncover what he means. "What about Ernesto? Do you think he was part of that . . . ambush? You feel we were suckers, feeding him, listening to his story?"

"Yeah. Made me mad. So," he shrugged. "Sorry."

"Ernesto didn't mean us any harm," I said. "He looked surprised at the end there. He didn't know what that Roscoe guy was talking about."

"You think so?"

"Oh, yeah. I was going to apologize to you, actually. We did the right thing, feeding Ernesto. He's okay. I was being an idiot because he . . . well, because he smelled bad."

Chris smiled slightly.

"And we sure did the right thing, getting away from those other guys, Roscoe and Dirtbag and them. Weren't they weird, those hoboes? Eh?"

"Yeah," he said.

"And that funeral – that was weird too. Not bad, like the hoboes, but weird. We've seen a lot of weird stuff today. Hey, Chris, do you remember what Ernesto said about us getting too old for the ravine? Do you think that's true?"

He waved a fly away from his juice box.

"I dunno," he said.

"You want to keep going?"

He nodded. "You?"

"Oh, yeah. Hey, Cory," I raised my voice. "Were you listening? You want to keep going on this trip, or do you want to stop now? What do you want to do?"

He thought for a moment, head to one side. "I want to pee," he said.

Come to think of it, so did I.

Chris, who was finishing his juice box, nodded thoughtfully. "Sounds like a plan."

Ah, the wonder, the freedom of being a boy in the solitude of the wilderness. Being able to gratify the simplest need effortlessly, whenever you wanted. It was a return to a primal state. Adam and Eve and Australopithecus.

Of course the best thing would be to pee off the raft. If you're a guy, you know this is true. Peeing off a moving vehicle? Does not get better, except maybe peeing off a high place. I remember once . . .

Skip it.

Anyway, we rounded a quiet bend and looked upstream and down. No one in sight. The trees grew close to the water's edge, the slope was steep.

I dropped the pole, and we lined up facing backward. We were just about to let the dogs out when we heard the rustling. It seemed to come from up ahead. I peered back over my shoulder but couldn't see anything. We were approaching a stretch of tired old willow trees that hung out over the creek.

"What was that?" I asked.

There it was again. Rustling and giggling. And I was sure I heard someone say, "Gross."

Was I imagining it? Chris had tilted his head to one side. "You heard that?" I asked him. He nodded.

Damn this ravine. Everywhere you turned there were people. Gangs, hoboes, mourners . . . what next? I still had to pee, but now I couldn't.

"If only I had an invisible helmet," said Cory.

"An invisible *helmet*?" I said. "What would be the point of that?"

"You know. Like that Greek guy had."

And then she descended. I'll never forget the sight. A shriek, and a slashing, slanting flight across our bow. From the willow ahead of us, a rope swung across the creek. At the end of the rope, a girl in a leopard-skin bathing suit thumbed her nose at us. She had tanned skin and flashing eyes and all the teeth in the world.

"Perverts!" she called as she swung across.

The rope had a knotted loop at the bottom. She had one bare foot in the loop. She faced us, hanging on with one hand, thumbing her nose with the other.

"Losers!" she called, swinging back. Her hair was short and blond and wild, like she'd combed it with her fingers.

We drifted toward her. She kept yelling at us. Chris grabbed the pole and held it like a quarterstaff. He looked shocked. He wasn't used to people calling him names. I have to say I didn't mind at all. Any time a stunning girl in a leopard-skin bikini wants to notice me, that's fine.

When the rope swung a second time, she leaped for the far bank, but her foot got caught in the loop. She fell awkwardly, on hands and knees, in some reeds. The rope drifted back.

"Ha!" Chris poled quickly toward her. When we ran aground, he jumped off.

"What are you doing?" I asked.

The girl cast a worried glance over her shoulder and tried to run. She couldn't put weight down on her bad foot and ended up dragging it after herself.

"Come on!" cried Chris. He waved me on from the bank, like a general urging a reluctant private out of the trench and into no man's land.

"Why?" I said.

"Don't argue, Jules. You're always arguing. She called us perverts."

"Yeah!" said Cory with a whoop. He charged into the underbrush. He didn't care why he was running. He hated being cooped up. When we played hide and seek, he always wanted to be it. On Crazy Hat Day at school, he wore a balaclava and charged from classroom to classroom, shouting, "It's a stickup!"

I shrugged and followed my friends. I didn't mind getting a closer look at this vision of a girl.

Oddly enough, we couldn't do it. She didn't have a big lead, but somehow we couldn't catch up. We'd glimpse her skin or her spots, and charge forward, but she'd be just as far ahead of us the next time we saw her.

"Where is she?" Cory asked, casting ahead.

We were more than halfway up the hill. I could hear the sounds from the world beyond the ravine. Lawn mowers, radios, cars. Splashes from someone's swimming pool. Expensive sounds. We were well south of the Elgin Avenue bike droppers. This section of the creek ran through money.

Chris pointed. She was leaning against a tree, panting. Her body drooped on its hinges like a badly hung door. When she saw us, she tried to run but ended up dragging herself along.

The way led through some low-growing underbrush. Chris took off, with Cory on his heels. Athletes. I was getting tired. And of course I still had to go to the bathroom. I kind of huffed and hobbled after them. I was way behind, focusing on my heaving lungs, when I heard shouts and a rustling and crackling sound. I looked up, and my friends had disappeared. A cloud of dust and leaves hung in the air.

Landslide, I thought.

Then I heard the giggles. I dropped to my knees and peered through the bushes. Not a landslide – a trap, like the ones they dig for tigers. I could see bare earth and an open hole. Leopard Skin and two other girls stood with their hands on their hips, looking down and laughing.

I tried to work out how old they were, using their bikinis as a guide. The youngest, in pink ruffles, would be five or six. Leopard Skin was older than I was by a year or two. Something about her said high school. The third girl might have been the same age as Leopard Skin but seemed older. She wore her polka dots like a bored top model, one hand on her hip.

"You can't climb out!" Leopard Skin called down into the pit. She didn't look injured or tired now. Her eyes flashed, and she skipped from foot to foot.

"Is this how you and Valerie play man trap, Miriam?" The girl in polka dots had hair out of a shampoo commercial. (You know the one – the model shakes her head slowly and this dark river of hair spills across the screen.) She spoke lazily, dragging the words from her mouth like a teenager from bed. "Why, these are just boys. Don't they look stupid! What do you think, Valerie, don't they look stupid?"

The little girl nodded and giggled into her thumb. She sucked it the way I used to, with her first finger wrapped over the top of her nose. She stayed well away from the edge of the pit.

Three girls in bikinis, laughing at Chris. When was the last time that happened? Part of me – I'm not proud of this – was pleased.

Another part of me couldn't stop looking at Miriam, the leopard-skin girl. Wow. A huntress. An Amazon. A comet, streaking across the sky of my delight. The languid older one was good-looking. But Miriam was, well, wow, like I said.

If only I were a Greek hero, I thought, I could rescue my friends, capture the girl, and show her who was boss. All those hero things. Mind you, if I were a Greek hero, I'd be taller and handsomer than I am. I'd have more muscles and less flab, and I probably wouldn't wear glasses. In short, I wouldn't be me. And that's who I was. What did I have going for me? A mind, of sorts. And a mouth, to talk with. I decided to use them.

I couldn't rescue my friends, so I did the next best thing. I betrayed them.

I stood up and walked forward through the under-brush, applauding.

"Great job." I smiled wide and unthreatening. "That was a fantastic trap, guys."

Funny how, if I call them girls, I'm making fun of them, but when I call them guys, it's a compliment.

"How long did it take you to dig the pit?" I asked.

"Who are you?" said the shampoo-commercial girl, showing Hollywood teeth.

"He's one of them," said Miriam, with her hand on the thumbsucker's shoulder. Protective. "He was on the raft. We forgot about him."

Hmm. Bet she wouldn't have forgotten about me if I had a magic sword.

I walked over to the pit and stared down. It was like a prison cell cut into the side of the hill – about six feet deep and steep-sided.

"She's right," I said. "You do look pretty stupid, don't you?"

Chris glared up at me.

"These guys sure made monkeys out of you."

"Let us out!" called Cory.

"Shh." I put my finger to my lips.

THE PARTY

CHAPTER 12 – *Pooh*

widened my smile even more and tried to put it into my voice. "Hi there," I said to the little girl. "How are you?"

She turned away and buried her head against Miriam. "Shy, eh?" I said. Miriam looked at me, like, *What the heck are you doing?* and patted the little girl's bare shoulder.

My smile was killing me. I turned to the languid one. "You know, that is a wonderful haircut."

She tossed her head, just like the commercial. Her hair flew around.

"D'you really think so?" Patting it back into place. Hair was a safe thing to admire. All she was wearing was two tiny pieces of cloth. I didn't want to get too personal. *Great polka dots you have there* might send the wrong message.

"Oh, yes. It's like a . . . mane."

"Huh?"

Miriam raised one eyebrow (I wish I could do that). "He's calling you a horse, Jasmine," she said. "Or a lion."

I laughed and said, "No no. I meant it as a compliment." I stayed with Jasmine. Couple of reasons for this. She seemed more important than Miriam. She moved slow. Her nails were perfect. Her makeup was fresh. She looked rich enough to own the ravine. Miriam, for all her energy, looked like a poor relation.

Also, I really liked Miriam, and the compliments were sort of crap, and I didn't want to lie to her.

We all wandered over to the edge of the pit. Cory was sitting down, but Chris was still on his feet, glaring upward. He had his arms folded over his chest.

"Tsk, tsk," I said.

He didn't say anything, but I could see his biceps bulge in anger.

Jasmine noticed too. "Ooh," she said.

Miriam bent beside the little girl. "Remember the story we read yesterday, Valerie?" she said. "Don't these two boys remind you of Pooh and Piglet? Remember when they were sitting in the pit, waiting for –"

"The heffalump," I finished.

Miriam straightened up, her hands on her hips in a "Get out of town!" gesture. A chance shaft of sunlight hit her, making the gem in her belly button flash. (How did I know her belly button was pierced? I was looking. Yes, even while I was trying to save my friends, and get us back on our journey, I was looking at a pretty girl's belly button. I don't defend this behavior, I simply note it.)

"You know that story?" she said. She raised her eyebrow again.

"It's one of my all-time favorites. Haff! Huff! A horrible heffalump!" I grinned at her. "So this is your cunning trap, eh? Did it take long to dig?"

"We found it like this, after the big storm last week. Valerie and I piled the dirt into a mound and left a hole in the middle. We called it a man trap. We didn't know we'd catch, well, heffalumps."

We laughed. The little girl too. "Heffalumps," she said and put her thumb back in her mouth.

"What's so funny?" asked Jasmine, with her eyes on Chris.

"You wouldn't get it," said Miriam.

So the gorgeous girl with the single raised eyebrow and the pierced belly button was also a Winnie the Pooh fan. It was official. I was in love. Nancy became a girl I'd eaten hot dogs to impress. This was the real thing.

Time to make friends. "I'm Jules," I said.

"Miriam." Her handshake was very firm. She had better muscles than I did. "And Valerie." I waved. She wiggled her baby fingers of her sucking hand. Looked like she was thumbing her nose at me. "Jasmine over there is Valerie's big sister. She and Valerie live up the hill."

"What about you?" I said.

"Oh, I'm just visiting my cousins here. I live out of town."

Ah ha! What did I say? Jasmine looked like she owned the ravine, and Miriam looked like a poor relation. Turned out I was dead-on. Sherlock Karapoloff.

"I want to apologize," I said. "The three of us live way upstream. We didn't mean to wreck your playground here by . . . uh –"

"Peeing in our creek?" said Miriam. Valerie giggled.

"Yeah. That was wrong," I said. "What can I tell you? We're guys. We thought it'd be fun. But we know better now."

Was that a smile on her face? It was.

"Tell you what," I said, moving over to include Jasmine. "Why don't you let my friends out? I'll vouch for them. How about if we never pee again? We'll be on our way in no time."

Jasmine was staring down at Chris. Was that a wave? Yes, it was. And a smile. And she was blushing.

"Jasmine!" called a voice from above. Not *above* like an angel from heaven, though. I meant *above* like at the top of the hill. "Jasmine, honey – your guests are here!"

Jasmine gestured to Miriam. They whispered together for a second. Miriam nodded and looked at me.

"Thanks, Mom!" Jasmine called back. "We'll be right up! Say, Mom – can I invite three more people?"

"I guess so. It's your party, honey. Do your guests have bathing suits?"

"Oh, yes."

And so, in the middle of our epic journey, we went to a party. Miriam and I pulled Chris and Cory out of the hole. Then Jasmine led us up the hill and into a fenced backyard. The ravine world was left behind as cleanly and completely as the Hundred Acre Wood when Christopher Robin goes upstairs to bed.

Cory drew me aside. "Do you smell fish?" he said.

"Uh . . . no. Do you?"

"No." He looked around. "There's worse places to be than here. I didn't like that hole much. Do you think they'll have a bathroom?"

"Yes." I stared at him. "Don't you dare use the pool."

For this was a pool party. A cool pool party. The sun shone on white decking, sun-screened bodies, and color-ful bathing suits. The guests were arriving fast.

Jasmine's mom met us just outside the door to the house. From a distance she might have looked like Jasmine's sister; but she didn't keep her distance. She got close. She took one look at Chris and smiled wide and white.

"Hello, big boy," she said, sliding next to him. "I'm so glad that my daughter invited you to the party. Can I get you . . . anything at all?"

She swirled the ice around in her drink with her finger, then licked her finger.

Chris took a step back. Jasmine sighed.

"I got to go to the bathroom," said Cory in a hoarse voice.

"Sure, honey." Jasmine's mom didn't turn her head. "Miriam, will you show this young man where to go? What about *you*?" she said to Chris, pulling on the last word to make it about a yard long. She was tall, like her daughter, and stared straight into his eyes. "Do you have to go to the bathroom too? I could show you the one next to my bedroom."

"Oh, Mom!" said Jasmine. "Leave him alone."

"My little girl." She put her free hand on Jasmine's shoulder. "I had her when I was a teenager myself. You know, you should greet your guests, honey. Suki and Sasha brought the cutest safari socks for a hostess gift. Go on," and she pushed her daughter away. "You," to Chris, and me, I guess, "make yourselves right at home. Have a swim. Get yourselves something to eat and drink. I'll be around to check on you. If there's *anything* you want, ask for Connie. That's me."

She let her fingers trail down Chris's arm.

Her bathing suit was white against her leathery brown skin. And minuscule. When she turned around I choked and looked up at the sky fast.

"A thong!" I whispered. "Jasmine's mom is wearing a thong! Yeesh!"

We were alone for the first time since the raft. He punched me. Hard.

"What are we doing here, Jules?"

"What do you mean? It's a party. We're having fun, I guess. I am, I know. Aren't you?"

"We should be on the raft. We're on a trip."

"This is a short break," I said. "We'll get back to the trip in a few minutes. And anyway, you were the one who got off the raft in the first place, chasing Miriam."

I rubbed my shoulder.

A girl in a wide-brimmed straw hat and wrap-around sunglasses came up and asked Chris if he remembered her from old Geenzie's science class last year. He shook his head. "Are you sure?" she said. He nodded.

I wondered if I could blend in. "Good old Geenzie," I said in a low voice. She ignored me.

"What about Liner's civics then? Didn't you sit beside that skank, Essy? I know we were in a class together," she said, "but I can't think whose."

Chris shrugged.

"Well, the safari is going to be something else, isn't it! Private guides through Amboseli, Ngorongoro. Amazing."

I bent toward the girl, ducking under the brim of her hat. Her face was a perfect oval, chin hardly noticeable. "What about me?" I said. "Do I look familiar too?"

I wasn't trying anything, just having fun.

She frowned. "I don't remember you around St. Wexler's."

"Oh, come on. What about those times with Mac?" All the nicknames, and the way she spoke and dressed, St. Wexler's had to be a private school. I was prepared to bet that somebody there would be named Mac.

"Mac?" she said.

"Yeah. Good old Mac . . ."

"Mac is the girl's wrestling coach."

Chris laughed. I struck a power wrestling pose with my arms in a circle. "Grr." The girl moved off, shaking her hat.

"I don't think I fooled her," I said.

"Why'd you call me stupid?" said Chris quietly.

"Huh? When?"

"When I was in that pit."

"I was just trying to get you out," I said. "And it worked, didn't it? I made friends with them, and here we are. Geez. Would you rather be back in the pit?"

"Nobody calls me stupid."

"Come on, Chris. I was just talking. And, let's face it, you were stupid to fall for Miriam's wounded bird act."

He punched me again. Ouch. "I hate her."

"What about the girl in the hat, there."

He snorted. "Her too."

"What do you think about . . . Connie? Because I think she's looking for you."

He shuddered.

CHAPTER 13 – *Whatever*

For a bunch of kids this was a very grown-up party. Hardly any splashing and screaming, no pushing at all. Mostly the guests smiled, sipped, and talked quietly, while the sun shone and the umbrellas flapped. They might have been their own parents. When I got out of the bathroom, Cory was waiting to go in and Chris was hiding from Jasmine's mom, so I was on my own. Conversation around me tended to be a bit cryptic. I pride myself on my ability to jump in and contribute, but it was hard to add anything to a discussion of old man Reynolds, and the time Boomer here did that thing with the ice cream scoop. I laughed along with everyone else in the group, but I didn't belong. When Boomer here – a beef-voiced guy with a square chin – mentioned the Serengeti, I said, "Ah, the 2.8 liter with the six forward speeds? I think my uncle has one of them." It didn't go over well. Boomer looked puzzled, and when I explained that I was making a joke, he turned his back. It's hard to get past other people's dislike. Maybe it was time to be moving on. I kept my eyes open for a chance to talk to Miriam, but she had taken little Valerie indoors.

"Drink, sir?"

I whirled. What a day – first *mister* and now *sir*. This was a grown-up in a white shirt and tie. He smiled and held out a drinks tray. "Shirley Temple or Coke?"

I didn't know what a Shirley Temple was. I took a Coke. "Thanks. I'm Jules," I said. The guy smiled and moved on. There was another shirt and tie across the pool, with another tray of drinks. They weren't guests, they were waiters.

I'd never been to a catered party before. I guess you don't introduce yourself to a waiter. Oh, well.

A splash from under the diving board and some applause. Miriam pulled herself out of the pool, shaking water out of her hair.

"Do another one!" someone called.

Miriam smiled, climbed back on the board.

"Who's *she*?" asked a girl from behind me in a high, breathy voice.

"Some poor cousin of Jasmine's, I think. She's visiting from out of town."

"Oh, I don't know about *poor*. That rhinestone in her navel must have cost at least $4.95."

The second voice sounded just like the first. I turned around. Two tall hairdos, two Shirley Temples, two pairs of identical sunglasses perched on two identical tip-tilted noses. Two outfits, no doubt expensive.

"Rhinestone! You should see the emeralds Jasmine has."

They laughed breathily together. I moved a few steps away.

Miriam ran to the end of the board, jumped hard, and launched herself into a perfect one-and-a-half, cutting the water without a splash.

More applause. When it died down, there was one of those silences you get at a party when everyone stops talking together. Everyone except the couple behind me.

"That suit is hideous!"

"But it's so perfect for her. A leopard. Ha ha. They should keep her in a cage, like a performing animal."

There was instant recognition. Everyone knew who they were talking about. Miriam stopped drying herself, and then started again. The breathy girls laughed together, realized that everyone was looking at them, and kept laughing anyway.

I went over to them. "Hello, there," I said, smiling pleasantly.

They gave me an up-and-down look, haircut to sand shoes, and back again. Their eyes were like cash registers, adding up how much I had cost. "Who are *you*?" said one, and "Where are you *from*?" said the other.

I thought of my Greek heroes. "I'm Nemesis," I said.

They giggled.

"And I come from far away. Say, I like your outfits."

"Really?" They forgot how inexpensive I was. A compliment is a compliment. Were they sisters? Clones? One of them had dark hair and wore a green-and-white-striped skirt and top. The other was blond in pink-and-white stripes.

"Absolutely. Best clothes at the party. I heard old Boomer say so." I edged toward them. "And . . . I don't mean to be personal, but your . . . profiles. Amazing."

"Oh?" They looked at each other, touched their noses self-consciously, and giggled. "Dr. Valvur," they said breathily.

"Huh?"

"He did our noses."

"Ah. Well, he did a great job."

"Nemesis is a funny name," said green stripes.

"It's Greek."

"Oh, Greek," said pink stripes. "Like the salad."

"Just like the salad," I said.

They giggled again, and Green Stripes touched my arm. Ah, Jules, you dog!

"Can I get either of you ladies another drink?" I asked.

They nodded, tipping their glasses up to drain them. I edged closer. Smiling as hard as I could, I put one hand on each of their backs and pushed them into the pool.

The waiters came around with long skewers of meat and a smelly sauce. I hesitated. "Come on, try one, Jules," said the one I'd introduced myself to.

"Um, all right," I said. "What is it?"

"Chicken. And it's tasty. Try the peanut sauce."

"Hey – that is good."

He nodded approval. "Try another – and get one for your girlfriend."

I turned around, and there was Miriam. I got a skewer for her.

"Now I can thank you twice," she said, taking a huge bite.

"Huh?"

"For this. And for what I saw you do to Bernadette and her friend."

The two breathy girls had hauled themselves out of the pool, spitting water, spitting mad. "Wait until my boyfriend gets here," said Pink Stripes. Now they were sitting at a patio table under an umbrella, clothes dripping, hair draggling down their backs, muttering together.

"Well, they were being mean," I said. "I thought you dived really well."

"They go to school with Jasmine. Private school, of course. As you figured out, everyone here is rich. They're all off to Africa next week on a school trip."

I nodded. Last school trip I was on we went to the museum. One of the guards found Cory halfway up the Tyrannosaurus rex, and we all got sent home. I tried to imagine Cory let loose on the plains of the Serengeti. I'd figured he'd either burn it down or be adopted by a pack of hyenas.

"They called you the poor cousin from out of town."

"That's me. My folks run a store in Ajax." She finished the meat, chewing hard. "My uncle Frank – that's Jasmine's dad – is some kind of jewel tycoon."

"Yeah, the girls were talking about her earrings."

"Jasmine's okay, considering how weird her mom is. Valerie's a sweetie. I'm here babysitting her. I don't fit in with Jasmine's friends, and that's okay."

I yawned elaborately. "I, on the other hand, am so charmingly adaptable that –"

"Oh, Jules, you belong here like a pork rind on a sundae."

"You calling me – ?"

"Look at you. Your shorts have a hole in one leg, your T-shirt is stained, and your glasses are crooked. And . . . is that an elastic band holding them on?"

I shrugged. "Hey, I'm from a different part of Scarborough. Doesn't mean I can't exchange views with old Boomer and the bimbo twins there."

Miriam's laugh was warm and appreciative. For a guy who tries to tell jokes, there is nothing better than an appreciative laugh. The mean girls' laughter sounded like snapping pencils. Miriam's was more like ice tinkling in a jug of lemonade.

I gazed at her while she filled my thirsty soul with her laugh. Her skin was as smooth as spread honey. No cracks, lines, pimples. Honestly, she was perfect. I was having a great time.

"Want another chicken skewer?" I said.

"Only if you will."

"Oh, I will."

Jasmine came up with a smile for me. "I'm so glad you guys came to the party," she said. "Your friend is amazing."

She went over to another group who were laughing together. "My nose is not that big," said a guy, holding up a napkin. More laughter, with Jasmine joining in.

"So is this a rich neighborhood?" I asked.

"It's Rouge Hollow," said Miriam. "This house is worth three million bucks."

"Ah, but does it have talking toilets?"

Chris came up, looking like the girl in the horror movie when the body falls out of the closet. "We've got to go, Jules," he said. "Now!"

"How come?"

"Connie," he whispered. Jasmine's mom.

"What about her?"

"There was a crowd in the kitchen. She grabbed me and pulled me down the hall. We ended up in her bedroom. She took off her . . . I mean, she turned around and I saw her . . . I mean, she had no . . ."

Chris didn't usually lose it like this.

"What?" I moved closer. "What did you see? What did she have? Tell me!"

"I can't talk about it. But we have to go now."

He looked shaken.

"Come on, Chris. This is a good party. Forget about Connie. That girl from old Geenzie's class liked you. And Jasmine was just by, talking about you."

"Jasmine? I've hardly seen her."

"Well, she said you were amazing."

Miriam had one eyebrow up. I looked for that spark that girls get when they're with Chris. She didn't seem to have it. And she stayed close to me. Usually when Chris and I are together, the girls are on his side.

"Let's get out of here," said Chris. "Come on. Back to the raft. If she catches me again –"

"You know, a lot of boys *like* Jasmine's mom," said Miriam.

"Do they? Well, I . . . oh crap!" He ducked and scuttled around behind me on his hands and knees, so that I was between him and the patio door. "There she is. I'll be hiding. Find Cory."

He scurried away, keeping his head down.

Miriam laughed. "Poor guy."

I'd never heard Chris called that before.

CHAPTER 14 – *Zombee*

The drinks and food kept coming. Miriam and I hung around together, sampling. (I was pleased – Nancy usually starts to wilt after she's been with me for a few minutes.) I told Miriam some of the things that had happened to us on our way down-stream. She thought Satan was a great name for a dog, but she didn't approve of the bike tossing off the Elgin Avenue bridge.

"What about the environment?" she asked. "All those broken bikes could be recycled."

"It's a ritual," I said. "Like a burial. These kids are saying good-bye to an old friend. When the dead Vikings got sent off to Valhalla with all their treasures, no one talked about recycling."

She considered this for a moment. "That's a stupid argument," she said.

"D'you think so? I was kind of proud of it."

I looked around for Cory, but I couldn't find him. I have to say, I didn't look very hard. I didn't want to leave the party yet.

Jasmine's mom came over to ask if I'd seen my "hunky friend." I shook my head.

When Connie walked away, I couldn't resist peeking, uh, behind her. Miriam noticed.

"She's too old for you, Chunky," she said. "And she's not interested."

Chunky.

"I'm not interested either," I said.

"Then why look?"

I shrugged. "I watch the luge racing at the Winter Olympics. Doesn't mean I want to strap myself to a sled and go. It's interesting to watch – but ridiculous. Kind of like Jasmine's mom, come to think of it."

Saying the word I got a weird vibe. *Mom.* I shuddered.

We ate more skewer things. These were shrimp. I was chewing away when I noticed Miriam looking me up and down. "What? Am I too chunky for you?" I asked. I was making a joke – I've been called worse names than Chunky.

"No, no. I like chunky," she said. "I eat a lot myself. But you eat as fast as you talk. When I saw you down in the ravine, I thought, This one won't shut up."

"You calling me . . . talkative?" I said, moving closer.

She wiped my lips with her napkin.

"*Psst.*"

We were standing near the side of the pool. I looked down, but the only person near us was what's-her-name, under the wide-brimmed straw hat. I went over, lifted the hat, and gasped. It was Chris, moving his arms and legs to look natural.

"There you are," I said. "Hey, don't I know you from old Ottley's class?"

"Have you found Cory?" he whispered.

"No. I'll keep looking."

I replaced the hat. Miriam laughed. I had a smile on, myself. Then, raising my eyes, I caught sight of Bernadette and her friend glaring from across the pool. My laughter dried in my throat.

We found Cory in the kitchen, a bright room with lots of gadgets. He was sitting at the marble counter, doing what he does at school all the time. Drawing. What do they call those portraits where you make the person look ridiculous? (Is my nose really that big?) Those things. He was doing them on napkins, with a Magic Marker. A girl sat in a tall metal bar stool chair, very self-consciously. Jasmine and a couple of other people were looking over Cory's shoulder.

He saw us and called out, "Hey, Jules. What do you call an undead bug with stripes?"

"I dunno."

"A *zombee*. Get it?" He drew a long, curving line on a napkin. "What does an undead ghost say?"

"Let me guess."

"*Zom-boo*! Ha ha ha ha."

The girl he was drawing laughed uproariously. Her eyes disappeared into her cheeks. Cory stared at her and made a couple of flicks with his marker.

"I want to go swimming," he said.

"Chris wants to leave soon," I said.

Jasmine's mom popped her head in the doorway.

"Chris? Did someone say Chris? Is he here?"

"Oh, Mother! Go chase someone your own age."

She waved her fingers at us and pulled the screen door behind her, calling, "You're as young as you feel, dear."

I laughed. Jasmine's eyes clouded over.

I wondered about that. If Jasmine's dad had been chasing after Miriam, I wouldn't have been laughing. So why was it okay to laugh at her mom? I decided that it wasn't okay. I shut up.

Miriam excused herself, saying she wanted to check on Valerie, and walked down the hall toward the bedrooms. Cory handed the napkin to the girl with the disappearing eyes, who laughed and showed it to Jasmine.

"*There* he is, Phil," said a high, breathy voice from the door. Bernadette, the pink-striped mean girl, stood in the doorway with her boyfriend. She pointed a finger at me, face thrust forward. Her boyfriend stared at me. And I at him.

"You?" he said, breaking into his wide, creepy smile. He saw Cory. "And him! Oh, this is perfect! Perfect!"

It was Daisy's brother, with the foxy face and the English accent. He'd changed his pants but still wore the baseball jacket and chain. This was the party he was dressed up for.

"He pushed me into the pool, Phil!" whined Bernadette. "The fat guy there."

"I prefer chunky," I said.

"He's the one, Phil."

"Oh, he's the one, all right," said Phil.

Not the way they said it in the *Matrix* movies.

Jasmine had a bright hostess smile on her face. I couldn't tell if she meant it or not – which I guess is the point of those smiles. "Phil Aherne! Glad you could make it! I see you know Jules already."

"Oh, yes, we're *old* friends."

His smile was as wide as hers (oh, those teeth of his) but easier to see through. I was reminded of those British movie gangsters who seem so jolly as they tell you in great detail how they are going to carve out your liver and feed it to you in slices, fried – no, not fried, because that would make it too tough. Poached, perhaps, in a red-wine reduction with fine herbs. They're funny, but scary too.

No reason why Phil couldn't go to St. Wexler. He was a rich guy, like the rest of them here. I wondered how he and old Boomer got along.

"I've been looking forward to the party all day, Jasmine," said Phil. "And now that I'm here, I couldn't be happier. I'm delighted to see Jules again. Especially since I brought my . . . new roommate. Jules hasn't met him yet."

Jasmine knew who he meant right away. Her smile disappeared and her eyes popped open. "Oh, Phil, you *didn't*! Not Bonesaw!"

"Oh, I did."

"But you said you wouldn't. You promised Bunky!"

"I couldn't resist. It's a pool party. He loves to swim."

Phil held out a small wrapped box. "These choco-lates are for you, Jasmine," he began, but she brushed past him on her way out the door.

I wanted to leave too, but Phil blocked my way. "You don't get to go yet," he said. "I'm not finished with you."

I held up my hands, placating. "Now, look –"

"No, *you* look." No placation going on here. "You look, Jules. You trespassed and insulted me at my house this morning. Now you've crashed my party and pushed my girl into the pool. I don't know *what* I should do to you."

He sounded as tough as he had when we first met. But I wasn't as scared of him now. He had no weapon, for one thing. And he wasn't surrounded by his friends. And, well, we were inside. For the life of me I couldn't figure out what he was going to do to me in Jasmine's kitchen.

I tried talking to him, like I had upstream. Not bab-bling from fear, more like I was reasoning with him. "About that pool thing," I said. "Normally I'd be as upset as you are. But, you see, I was in a pickle myself. Your girlfriend had insulted –"

"Phil!" Bernadette pouted. You don't see too many pouts. "This guy talks all the time. Can you shut him up?"

"Yeah, baby," he said.

"Hey, you sounded exactly like Austin Powers, there," I said. "He says *Yeah, baby* just like that."

Phil stepped right up to me. His chin was one inch from mine. His eyes were blue and sparkly, like the water when the sun hits it. Interesting, and kind of unsettling. I hadn't completely lost my fear of him – here it was again.

Without turning his head, he said, "Get Colin and Zach, baby."

"Okay." She turned in the doorway. "Bonesaw too?"

"Not yet."

She left.

Phil was way too close to me. My stomach sticks out a little past my chest, and his chest stuck out past his stomach, so we were like a couple of joined jigsaw puzzle pieces. "Sorry about the Austin Powers line," I said. "It was pretty cheap. It just popped out. I didn't mean to make fun of you."

"Shut up."

"It's just that I –"

"Shut up, I said."

Well, enough already. He was trying to push me around, intimidate me. There comes a time when you have to push back. I used my stomach.

"Where do you think you're going?" His voice grated.

Why wasn't I as scared as I had been two seconds ago? This was interesting. Because I was starting to get mad? Maybe.

"I'm going to say good-bye to my hostess, Phil. Then I'm collecting my friends and heading back down to the ravine. Our trip's almost over. We can't be more than a half hour from the lake. There's a park down there. When we get to the park, I'll call home, and we'll get picked up." I nodded to myself. "Yeah, that's it for now. That's where I think I'm going, Phil."

He did the last thing I expected. (All right, maybe not *the* last thing. He didn't disappear, or turn into a giraffe, or do that *Exorcist* bit where his head spins around and around. But he did surprise me.) He laughed.

"Rafting," he said.

"What?"

"Such a lame idea. How old are you – eleven?"

"Thirteen," I said, and wouldn't you know it, my voice cracked on the word. Not on my long speech, but on the one word. Puberty is a pain, I tell you.

"Thir-*teen*?" he mimicked. "Thir-*teen*? That's hilarious. No wonder you're doing a lame raft trip."

"Shut up," I said. He was starting to get to me.

"Thirteen! You're such a baby. Do you guys have a clubhouse too? Those are cool, aren't they? A secret place with no girls allowed?"

I didn't say anything. I thought about our Dun Killin hideout. Maybe it was a little lame at that. But it was ours. How dare he make fun of it.

"The ravine!" He laughed again. "You know where I'm going next week? East Africa. That's right: East Africa. Where the crocodiles are. Now that is a trip for grown-ups. Piddling around on a raft is for kids like you."

It was like there was a teeter-totter inside me, with two Juleses tipping back and forth – Scared Jules and Angry Jules. Now Scared Jules was at the bottom and Angry Jules was on top. I was mad.

"You shut up!" I said.

His trip *was* cooler than ours. But hearing Phil talk about our trip, calling it lame, made me more committed to it. I was determined to finish. And, along the way, I really wanted to show Phil what I thought of him.

"Yeah, the ravine is full of people doing lame things," I said. "You know what's really lame? Beating up hoboes. That's what you do, isn't it? Wander around the ravine and pick on poor gomers who can't fight back. That's real lame, Phil. And it's mean."

I couldn't make him mad. He shook his head and did that *phht* thing. "Don't be such a little pissy pussy."

"A what?"

"We're just having fun. And it's not as if these guys are normal people. They're practically zombies, lurching around down there."

"Zombies?"

We'd got Cory's attention. He'd been zoning out, staring at the counter, maybe trying to decide what color it was. Now he was back. "What about zombies?"

He noticed Phil for the first time. "Hey, I remember you," he said. "You're the guy who has to babysit his little sister and brother!" He laughed. "When did you get here? Do you still swing like a girl?"

Honestly, you got to love Cory.

Caricature. *That's the word I was looking for – the drawing that Cory was making, where all the facial features are exaggerated. Funny that I couldn't think of it until I got back home, especially if you remember that I was able to come up with Nemesis, the Greek figure of vengeance. I picture her with a cape and muscles. Which is odd, because, if you think about it, Nemesis is often a slow and painful death from a crippling disease. Not a cape-wearing kind of a moment.*

I'm back at Dun Killin on one of those days of steady summer rain that won't turn into a storm and won't let up until tomorrow. Drip drip drop little August shower. (Chris can't stand that movie, "Bambi's mom dies!" he says, but I like it. Sorry, getting off topic again.) My running shoes are soaked and muddy, and my pen won't write very well because of the water on the notebook. Yeck. I'll probably head home soon. I think Baba is making zelnik for lunch – that's a kind of Macedonian sandwich, only with pastry instead of bread.

Cory's good at caricature. You should see his picture of Detective Strongman, the cop who asked us all the questions about the fire. Cory made him look like a farm horse, except for the glazed zombie eyes.

Back to Jasmine's party now. By the kitchen door, Phil and I were locked eye to eye and, uh, front to front – think of

*the way South America fits into Africa. He still held his hostess
gift. Over by the counter, Cory was laughing. Out by the pool,
the catered summer afternoon was being ruined by the mysterious Bonesaw.*

Miriam came in, whistling. She'd changed her clothes
and done something to her hair. I liked it – whatever it
was. I liked her outfit too. Shorts and a tank top. I waved.
She raised her eyebrow.

"I know you," she said to Phil. "You're a friend of
Bunky's."

"Bunky?" I said.

"Jasmine's brother." Maybe she colored slightly. I
thought about names. Geenzie. Bunky. Boomer. Who
were these guys?

Phil moved away from me to glare at Cory. "You
shut up!" he called.

But of course he didn't. There was no Scared Cory
inside him. He laughed harder than ever. Phil got so mad
his hand trembled, and when the kitchen door behind
him swung inward, striking his arm, he let go of the
hostess gift. The small wrapped box skittered across the
floor toward Cory, who pounced like a mongoose.

"Sorry!"

My waiter pal ducked his head around the door,
wearing a professional smile. "Sorry. I didn't see you standing there, sir. Didn't mean to hit you. My mistake, sir."

He came into the kitchen carrying an empty tray. "I
came in to get some more chicken satay. Folks out there
seem to really go for it."

Cory held up Phil's box of chocolates. The moment froze. It was like we were posed for the cover of a Hardy Boys book. *The Gift Box Mystery*. Everyone focused on it.

The waiter broke the spell, moving to the fridge for a plate of skewered meat with sauce. He put it in the microwave, smoothed down his apron, and smiled at us all. There was a scream from outside, followed by a splash. And another scream. And a new sound, faint, but getting louder. A siren. The waiter's smile didn't change.

Phil, hand still shaking, pointed at the box. "Give that back!" he said.

Cory pulled open the elastic waist of his shorts and dropped the gift inside. His face cracked like an egg into a big white smile. I knew what he was going to say before he said it.

"You want it? Come and get it!"

I'd laughed with the supply teacher and the squirt gun because, well, there's just something funny about a guy hiding a foreign object in his pants. But this was different. "Cory – no!" I said. "Do you want chocolate down there?"

He stopped laughing and threw the box back on the floor just as Bernadette came in from outside. With her was a familiar guy in a black baseball jacket and a nose ring. Colin.

"What a party!" he was saying. "Bonesaw doesn't want to get out of the water. People are screaming and calling the cops. Did you see Zach necking with Jasmine's mom? Lucky guy, and he never even met her before. I've always thought she was hot, for an older –"

He stopped when he caught sight of Cory and me.

"*You guys?*" he said. "What are you guys doing here?"

The microwave pinged, and the waiter took out his plate of chicken satay.

"I still don't understand about the zombies," said Cory. I shushed him, pulling us both toward the inside of the house. Scared Jules was back. There was something in the way Phil stared at Cory. He looked crazy enough to do anything. The air crackled with tension.

Miriam felt it too. She was on my other side. "Chunky?" she whispered, grabbing my hand. "What's going on here?"

Cory, of course, was oblivious. It amazed me that he could go through life as noisily as he did and not realize the effect he had on people. He had no idea that Phil hated him. No idea at all. I remembered him hitting rocks with my tennis racket after I'd told him not to and then being surprised when I was upset. *You broke my racket*, I said. *Uh huh*, he said, *and are you going to eat all of that Snickers?* There was no cause, with Cory, and no consequence. As far as he was concerned, other people's actions or reactions were part of a totally random and mysterious universe. The only person I'd ever known him express any feeling about was his mom.

"So, do you guys *know* any zombies?" he said to Phil and Colin. "Have you seen any, down in the ravine? Up where we live, we thought we saw a zombie once, but it turned out to be a dummy. You know, one of those scarecrow things they put out for Halloween. It was lying on the ground." He sighed. "Boy, I'd sure like to find a zombie."

They shuffled across the kitchen toward us, hunched slightly, hands stretched out. Bernadette stayed a step behind them, smiling meanly over their heads. Were they planning to grapple us to the death? Drag us out to meet Bonesaw? I didn't like it one bit. But I didn't know what to do except back up.

"Psst!"

The whisper came from the darkened hall behind me. I peered over my shoulder. Chris's head poked out of a doorway on the left. He beckoned.

Good enough. I kept hold of Miriam's hand, grabbed Cory by the shirt, and ran.

"What's going on?" said Cory. "I don't –"

I pushed him down the hall ahead of me.

"Git 'em, boys!" cried Bernadette, a phrase bringing back such strong memories that I turned around to stare.

The boys were coming. But they had to get past the waiter first.

"Chicken, gentlemen?"

The waiter was on the small side, though I had already noticed his large, muscular hands. His white apron was wrapped around his skinny hips and tied in a neat bowknot. He was not physically commanding, and yet there was something about his voice that stopped Phil

and Colin in their tracks. He was like a sorcerer who had
them in thrall. They could not rush past him. "It's very
good chicken," he said. "I recommend that you try some."
And they stopped, as though they had run into a wall.

Phil growled something in a low voice and reached
out his hand. I saw a guy on TV get hypnotized once. Phil
moved like him.

"Thank you, sir," said the waiter. "And here's a
napkin. How about you, sir?"

"Um . . . I guess so." Colin took a skewer and a
napkin as well.

"Git 'em!" cried Bernadette.

The waiter ignored her. "Careful, gentlemen," he
said. "It's hot."

Chris let us into a bedroom with lacy pink everything
and locked the door behind us. The smell was sweet and
perfumy. The bed was round and unmade. There was a
mirror on the ceiling over it.

I didn't have to ask whose room it was. "So this is
where you went with old Connie," I said. "Where she
took off her –"

"Yes."

Funny guy, Chris. At school he has girls hanging off
him and he doesn't care. He'd rather play football.
Jasmine's mom really upset him. Me, I agreed with Colin.
I thought she was strange, but, well, interesting.

I told Chris that Bonesaw was here, along with the
guys in the baseball jackets.

"I *knew* it!" he said.

"Quiet." Miriam stood with her ear to the door. "I think they're coming."

"Let's go," whispered Chris. He showed us a window that opened onto a balcony.

"Looks good," I said. "We can climb down to the side yard. Cory, come on!"

He was lying on the bed, waving up at the mirror. Chris shuddered.

"If you're so grossed out, why did you come back here?" I asked him.

"Figured it was the last place she'd look."

"Shhh," Miriam grabbed my arm and pointed. The door handle wiggled up and down and then stopped.

"Are they going away?" I whispered doubtfully.

"Maybe they're getting Aunt Connie."

"Hurry!" said Chris.

We dragged Cory to the window and threw open the filmy curtains. The balcony was only a few feet off the ground. Romeo would have no trouble climbing into the bedroom. (And if Jasmine's mom was Juliet, she'd probably help him.)

To the left was the backyard. To the right, through a gate, was the street. Miriam checked both ways to make sure no one was watching. "Leave one at a time," she whispered. "Get to the front of the house. There's a public entrance to the ravine a few doors down."

"Meet at the raft in . . . ten minutes," I said, checking my watch. "It's two thirty-one now."

"I don't have a watch," said Cory.

"Then you can go first."

Chris and I each took an arm and lowered him to the ground. "Count to six hundred, slowly," I said.

"One . . . two . . . three . . ." He trotted toward the gate.

Miriam pointed at Chris. He nodded and executed a perfect vault over the balcony, landing gracefully on his feet. He waved and ran off.

My turn now. I had my hands on the balcony railing. Time to get back on track, I thought. Back to the raft, and my friends. Back to the ravine.

I looked over my shoulder. Miriam lifted an eyebrow and beckoned.

"Hey, there," she whispered.

Friends and safety pulled me in one direction. *Get out of here!* they seemed to say. This girl pulled a different way. I was torn between past and future – but not very deeply, and not for long. I mean, you've always got the past, right? You can visit there anytime you like. But you only have one future at a time. I turned with a smile.

"Well, *hello*," I said. And for once my voice did not betray me.

CHAPTER 16 – *Romance*

I stepped back inside the perfumed bedroom. The curtains blew gently. My heart was galloping. My skin felt hot all over. For the first time in my life I was alone with a beautiful girl who liked me. I wanted to say something romantic and sexy, but my mind was a blank. Think, Jules, think.

"Uh, what do you put on your hot dogs?" I asked finally.

"Huh?"

"I dress mine like a traffic light, with the ketchup at the top and the relish at the bottom, and the mustard in the middle."

"Oh, Chunky!"

Miriam held out her arms. We moved together, drawn by a force stronger than either of us. Our hands found their way to each other. That doesn't sound right. Our hands found each other's hands. Still not right. Our fingers . . . skip it. We clasped each other tightly. There we go. Her eyes melted into mine. Our lips met. And time stood still.

All the love songs are really about this moment.

When we drew apart, we were both breathing hard.

"Wow," I said, pushing my glasses up.

"Me too, Chunky. Me too."

"Piglet was right. It really is better with two," I said.
She laughed.

"I've never kissed anyone before. Not like *that*," I
said.

"Uh huh," she said.

"Have you kissed anyone like that?"

"Hmm?"

"I said, have you –"

"Come here, you." She put her hands up to my face
and pulled me toward her.

Time to go. We exchanged numbers and addresses, and I
jumped off the balcony, landing not nearly as gracefully
as Chris. I looked up at the window, but she was gone. I
took a deep breath and laughed it out.

To me, things aren't all funny or all solemn but a
mixture of both. Same way people aren't all bad or all
good. So the scene with me and Miriam was funny and
serious together. I laughed, but even as I laughed I knew
I would never forget that moment with her. A hundred
years from now, on my deathbed, surrounded by people I
love that I haven't met yet, I'll still be able to call up every
detail of my first real kiss. I'll remember the perfume and
the curtains blowing, and my friends outside. I'll remember the smell of her hair, the feel of her eyelashes on my
cheek, the softness of her tongue.

I meant it. All the love songs.

CHAPTER 17 – *Complications*

Jasmine lived on one of those curvy crescents. Manicured lawns, cobbled driveways, and perfectly enormous homes. The monster across the street had a turret and slit windows, and a metal fence with spikes to stick the heads of your enemies on.

Two police cars were parked in Jasmine's driveway, lights flashing and static crackling from their radios. A crowd of people stood nearby, shaking their heads and muttering disapproval. A woman with a twin stroller was complaining to a man with a collie dog. "You'd think this was one of those Asian gang neighborhoods," she said and then, "Oh, sorry! I didn't mean it that way."

"Uh huh," said the collie man, who looked Asian.

The twin-stroller lady frowned and moved off. I hoped she was embarrassed.

I wondered what the dog would do if I called out, *Hey, Satan*.

I edged through the crowd. They were more dressed up than the folks in my neighborhood were, and they smelled nice, like flowers and pine trees and musk and sea mist. (My mom bought my dad some cologne once. He thought it was mouthwash and tried to drink it. It burned so bad he spat it all over the bathroom mirror and poured the rest of the bottle down the sink.)

One of the cops was on the walkie-talkie to someone he called sarge. Great accent he had, from Texas or
someplace down there.

"Yep, there's a pool party here, sarge," he said. He
pronounced it *heah*. "But with a difference."

He listened, then said yep again.

"Ain't never seen a boy this big, sarge. He won't
come out the pool – and I cain't get him out."

Bonesaw, I thought.

"Cain't tell you, sarge. No one's talking. The home-
owner's in hysterics. Most of the kids is goin' home. I
don't blame 'em."

I wondered if the cops would get around to arresting
Bonesaw or if they would just throw him out. They
couldn't charge him for swimming, could they?

"Yep," the cop said again. Not much for questioning authority. A real yep man.

"You'd think this was one of those gang neighborhoods," said a familiar voice. She'd found someone else
to spew at. "Police cars, noisy parties. My God, it's so
embarrassing. Next thing you know we'll be on the six
o'clock news. *Beatrice! Benedict!* Stop it!" Her twins were
fighting in the stroller, pulling each other's hair and
screaming. Gangsters in the making.

Kids, your mom is a dork, I thought.

I found the path down to the ravine. Within seconds
the forest closed behind me, and the street was gone. I
forgot about the bigoted lady and the cops and the party.
I even forgot, momentarily, about Miriam. I was back in

the woods, surrounded by the smell of dirt and flowers, the sound of birds and water. I moved through shadow and dappled sunlight, over rocks and fallen logs. Downward, ever downward, to the creek. A blue jay called overhead. I peered up but couldn't find him. I wondered if he was eating bees. They do that, you know. Snap them up in their beaks like cocktail peanuts.

Chris was sitting on a rock with his back against a tree and his feet on the beached raft. Like me, he looked happier to be back down here. He was whistling softly to himself as I came up. I recognized the tune.

"Did you have any trouble getting away?" I asked.

He shook his head. "Crowd in front of the house."

"Did you see the police cars? I heard one cop talking about a boy in the pool. Too big to drag out, he said. I figure he was talking about Bonesaw."

Chris frowned. "Bonesaw. Where'd those guys go – Phil and them?"

"I don't know. I didn't see them."

I wondered why he was so grumpy. I was feeling pretty good.

"Nice down here, isn't it?" I said. "That party was fun, but I'm glad to be back."

I waded out to Miriam's rope swing. Jumped up and hung there for a few seconds, swaying back and forth.

"*Fun*?" Chris looked like he'd bitten into a rotten apple.

"Well, some of it."

"*You* may have had fun. You and –"

"Miriam," I said.

"Yeah. What kind of name is that?"

"I don't know. It's her name. She's okay. What kind of name is Jasmine? Or Christopher, for that matter. Geez, man."

He went back to his whistling.

"Catchy tune," I said. It was the one Randy's mourners were singing.

He stopped abruptly.

I got out the map, unfolded it. Chris stood up and stretched, facing away from me. I knew he was embarrassed. I traced our route down the creek. We'd come a long way. Another thumb length or so and we'd be at the lake.

"Sorry, Jules," Chris said quietly. "For talking about what's-her-name that way – Miriam. I was being –"

"Stupid?" I didn't look up.

"Yeah."

He came around to stare over my shoulder. "There." He pointed. "Highway 2. Walter said we'd see it next. You know, we're practically there."

"Walter? Oh, yeah. Him."

I put away the map. The wind began to strengthen, blowing down the ravine. Miriam's rope creaked, swinging on its own from the willow fork. The long streamers of leaf were silver side up.

"Where's Cory?" Chris asked.

Good question. He'd had plenty of time to get here, even for him, allowing for him to get distracted by the color of a toadstool.

"We should never have let him go by himself," he said. "It was that Miriam girl's idea."

I frowned. "She was trying to stop us from being found out."

"She was trying to get you alone, Jules."

He sounded like my mom when my dad works late and they have to go to a party.

"Shut up, Chris. Are you saying it's *my* fault that Cory is missing?"

"Yes. No. I don't know."

"'Cause it isn't."

"I want to finish the trip," he said.

"Me too. Let's find Cory and get back to it."

We went looking for him. I wanted to split up, but Chris convinced me that we were better together. "That way we won't have to find each other."

We put the knapsack back under the raft and retraced our steps, casting left and right into the bushes. We checked the hole that Cory and Chris had fallen into. We crisscrossed the eastern slope of the ravine. We didn't find him. We shouted his name. The wind, growing stronger, carried our words away, but brought none back to us.

Halfway up the slope was a pine tree caught in the act of falling. The bottom roots clung firm. The tree stuck out of the hill like a . . . well, like a diving board. We edged our way out and peered into the ravine below.

"There he is!"

Chris pointed. I saw the red cap clearly against the

dark green foliage. He was jogging parallel to the creek. How had we missed him? How had he not heard us?

"He's moving away from the raft," I said. "He's lost."

"Cory!" shouted Chris.

The red cap kept moving.

"Cory! Cory!"

"He's not paying attention," I said. "What an idiot."

Chris leaped off the sticking-out tree and charged downhill.

"Watch for holes," I called.

We caught up to the red cap in a minute. It was Cory's all right. I recognized the cheesy logo. But it wasn't Cory in the cap.

INTERRUPTION Number 2 – Git 'em, boys!

Top-five family memories. I'm not talking about the trip to Disneyland or the birthday you got a pony – I mean everyday memories. Throw your mind back and think about things that you love doing with your family. Making cookies and eating the dough. Playing catch in the park. Kite flying. Going out for ice cream. Board games that last for days. You know the sort of thing.

Can you think of five? Can you think of any? I asked Cory once, and he shrugged his shoulders. *My mom found a mouse in the kitchen cupboard,* he said, *and let me kill it.* I patted him on the shoulder. That's great, I said. A nice, warm Hallmark kind of moment.

All right, mine would be:

5. Cards. We play poker for pennies after dinner. My mom's a good bluffer. OMIGOD, she'll say, picking up her cards. And I won't know if she really means it.

4. Cartoons with Dad. I usually sleep late now, but when I was younger, Dad and Julie and I would eat cereal and watch really early, really bad shows. He'd laugh harder than either of us.

3. Christmas Eve. I prefer it to Christmas Day because it's all still ahead of you. Hope and no presents is better than reality with presents that are all a size too small. Julie and I exchange our gifts then. One year she got me a bag of elastics and I got her a teacup. We spent hours shooting my present into hers.

2. Dinnertime. All of us around the table and stuffed peppers coming up. Or chicken with onions. Rice pudding for dessert. Dad wiping his face and calling for seconds. How can you beat that?

And my number-one family memory, the one that I'll take with me longer than anything else I've ever experienced – anything good, that is, don't get me started on my family nightmares – is . . .

1. Storytime. Which is the point of this interruption. I loved having Dad read to me, largely because he loved it too. He'd sit on the bed in his cardigan, begin real calm and then get more and more excited as the story unwound. When he got to the climax of the heffalump story in *Winnie the Pooh*, he'd be bouncing up and down on the bed, and I'd be laughing until the tears ran down my face.

Mom was all, *Jules is so smart, you should be reading him Alice In Wonderland.* But Dad read what I wanted to hear. One winter when I was four or five, I got addicted to *Rustlers of Grim Gulch.* He read it over, and over, and over. And over. And he enjoyed it every time. Only thing I remember from the story now is the stagecoach being ambushed, and the chief bad guy yelling, *Git 'em, boys!* to the rest of the gang. Dad loved that line. He'd leap from the bed and wave his hand in the air, firing off an imaginary six-shooter.

So when Bernadette yelled it in Jasmine's kitchen, I thought of my dad. In fact, writing this now, I can call up the scene clear as anything. A winter evening, crisp and cold outside, with the sound of traffic muted through the storm windows. Me under the covers in my yellow flannel pajamas and my dad, my crazy, uncombed dad, in slippers and cardigan, clutching the tattered storybook with the brown cover, his eyes blazing, yip-yipping and yee-hawing, capering around my bedroom as if on horseback, the very model of a cattle rustler in the Old West.

THE CHASE

CHAPTER 18 – *Back to the story*

The guy wearing Cory's cap was an old hobo, dressed in a shirt and pants that had once been off-white but were now off-off. He sank to his knees when we caught up to him. Chris tore the cap off angrily.

"Where'd you get this?" I asked.

The creek rippled quietly nearby. The blue jays called. The leaves rustled. The hobo covered his head with both hands and sobbed.

"Spare me! I . . . found the cap, as you found me. And I took it – a sin. Be sure your sin will find out, says the Book. On the ground I found it, where it lay. From the boy's head it fell, when they dragged him off. Oh please spare my white hairs and aging bones and sinews."

He peered up at us.

"Where is your jacket?" he said to Chris.

"Jacket?"

He peered closer.

"So . . . you are not like them," he said.

He could have been a televangelist, except for sounding scared. Televangelists aren't scared of anything. This guy had white hair on the parts of his head that weren't bald and scabby. His eyes oozed when he blinked.

"Like who?" I asked.

"The ones who took the boy away."

"What boy?" I was getting confused.

"The one in the cap. Who else are we talking about? Those who took him wore the black jackets and uttered the name of power. All around him they were, like the troops of Midian, and they took him away as they took our Lord Jesus away. Jesus did not have a red cap, but the boy did, and when it fell, I took it to cover my poor burnt head."

Chris and I looked at each other. Black jackets had to be Phil and the gang. They hadn't wasted any time outside Jasmine's mom's bedroom. They'd left the party, gone straight to the ravine, and waited for us. They knew what our raft looked like. Cory came first, and they took him. He'd be the one they wanted most, anyway – the one who'd made Phil so mad.

The hobo shifted on the ground. "May I get up, please? My knees are sore."

The Jesus talk made me uncomfortable, but I couldn't let an old man kneel on the ground in front of me. That was wrong. I felt bad enough to offer an arm to him. He thanked me and climbed up my arm to his feet. That sounds funny, doesn't it?

"Any bets on the name of power?" I asked Chris.

He thought for a moment, and nodded.

"Bonesaw."

"That *name!*" The hobo fell back against the nearest tree. Liquid poured from his eyes.

"Damn!" Chris clenched his fists together on the cap.

I understood. "You're the one they call the Preacher, aren't you?"

The hobo peeked through his fingers at me.

"Ernesto told me about you, and the others who have been beaten up by the Bonesaw gang. My name is Jules and this is Chris. We want to find our friend. Can you help us?"

He shook his head weakly.

"Come on, Preacher. What does Jesus say? *An enemy of my enemy is my friend.* You don't like Bonesaw and neither do we. Help us. And we will revenge you. And" – remembering Ernesto – "we have some oatmeal cookies left."

He dropped his hands. "Food?"

"Not just food – these are my mom's cookies. You can have some. But first show us where you found the cap."

He trotted back toward the raft without another word. We followed. The people who say time is money are all old and rich. For the rest of us, food is money. I couldn't have offered the Preacher any amount of time that would have meant as much to him as a cookie. (Come on now, would you rather turn the clock back two weeks or find a chocolate bar in your pocket? Exactly.)

There was a well-worn path beside the creek. The going was easy. Really, it was a wonderful afternoon to be outdoors. I would have enjoyed it, except for this hole inside me – Cory was gone. I couldn't help thinking of the way Phil had looked at him. Something not right there. Cory was like a little kid. I felt responsible for him. And now he was gone. Damn it. Damn it.

Chris was frowning. "You know, Jules, Jesus never said anything about an enemy of my enemy."

"I must have heard it in an old Clint Eastwood movie," I said.

"Here" – the Preacher stood in a clearing near the raft with his arms spread wide – "were two in their black jackets with the snaps on the front. Here also was the boy in the red cap. I was sleeping there." He pointed at a clump of bushes with a curved brown fingernail. "The Book says to be ready for you know not when the master will come home, even in the middle of the night, but I was weary and I slept. When I heard the voices, loud and mocking, I awoke. I saw the black jackets, and I was afraid." He touched the bald side of his head. "They mocked the boy in the cap, even as the mob mocked the Lord Jesus. They struggled with him and stripped him of his cap. Like Jesus, the boy did not resist. He smiled on them and suffered them to lead him up the hill." The Preacher pointed across the creek. "I took his cap to cover my burnt head, and went on my way."

He took another cookie, his third, and began to gnaw it.

"Doesn't sound like they dragged him away, kicking and screaming," I said to Chris. "He just went along with them. I wonder how they got him to go?" Then I thought, Was Phil even here? The Preacher had only talked about two black jackets. Maybe Phil and Bonesaw had stayed at the party.

Chris shrugged. "Doesn't matter why. He's gone. We have to get him back." He spoke casually, but I knew he'd never quit. It was the *said I would* side of him.

I swatted a bug that was trying to settle down and raise a family on the inside of my elbow.

"Okay," I said. "Should we call the cops?"

"No." Chris took the knapsack from me. "No evidence except the Preacher guy, and he says Cory went off on his own. Cops won't do anything."

That sounded right. "So who are you calling?"

He had the cell phone at his ear. "Home."

He talked longer than usual – almost a moment. I think he was feeling shaky. The whole episode with Jasmine's mom – which was *mostly* funny to me – might have hit him hard. He hadn't been very nice about Miriam, which wasn't like him. And now Cory was missing. "Yeah, me too, Mom," he said. "Nice to talk to you. I'll call soon."

For Chris, practically an epic.

He hadn't said anything about Cory to his mom. I didn't want to tell my folks either. As long as they didn't know about the problem, it didn't exist. But we had to do something, and soon. Chris thought so too.

"Let's go." He handed the knapsack to me.

"Where?"

"After them! They went up the hill. Let's follow them!" He was ready to take off right now.

"What'll we do at the top of the ravine? Which way will we go?"

Chris didn't say anything.

"Let's see if we can get more information first. Then maybe we'll know where to go."

I've read enough mystery stories to know that you have to question witnesses thoroughly. They always see more than they think they do. So as the Preacher massaged his cookie with grizzled jaws, I asked him about the characters with the jackets.

Did one of them have a bandana? I asked. Oh, yes, he said.

Did the other have a nose ring? Verily, he said.

And there were only two of them? In truth, only two, he said.

I asked if there was anything else he remembered about the conversation. A name, a street? Anything at all?

He shook his head.

Chris was watching carefully. His hands were fists. Not that he wanted to beat the information out of the Preacher. It was a kind of moral support, I suppose. He was *willing* the Preacher to remember.

"Okay, then," I said. "What was the last thing they said?"

He looked blank.

"Go back to the scene. You're sitting in the bush, listening. What was the last thing anyone said? The last thing you heard as they started to walk away with Cory? Think hard, Preacher. How do you feel? You're relieved, aren't you, because they are walking away?"

"Yes."

"And you see that cap on the ground. Cory's red cap. You want it to cover your head from where they burnt you."

"Yes."

"So . . . what are they saying?"

The sky was starting to cloud up. The forecast this morning had said ten percent chance of showers. This was the ten percent.

The Preacher shook his head. "Nothing," he said. "Sorry. I can hear the boy who had the cap. I hear his voice, but not the other ones."

"Okay, that's our friend Cory. What's he saying?"

The Preacher closed his eyes. "He's telling . . . a joke. Yes. A joke about an undead man going into a bar."

I nodded. Sure sounded like Cory.

"And then . . ." The Preacher opened his eyes wide. "He said a number."

"Who?"

"The one in the bandana. He didn't guess the answer to the joke. He said a number to his friend. I hear it now, ringing in my head like a gong. Seventy-four. He says to his friend, 'Seventy-four.' Like that. And the friend nods. And the boy in the cap laughs and says, 'No no. He orders a *zombeer*.'"

"Seventy-four," I said. "Are you sure?"

"Yes. I didn't remember it until now. But it's true."

So the mystery stories were right.

"What's seventy-four mean?" asked Chris.

"O God, why hast thou cast us off for ever?" said the Preacher. "Why doth thine anger smoke against the sheep of thy pasture?"

"Huh?" I said.

"Psalm Seventy-four. The first verse."

"Ah. Thanks." But I had a different idea.

"Can I have the cap?" the Preacher asked.

"Let's give it to him," I said. "He did help us." Chris nodded. I dug it out of the knapsack, along with my mom's plastic container. "Have another cookie too," I said. "You can't eat a cap."

We followed the trail of the three boys. It actually was a trail. The grass was trampled and bushes bent back. We followed it up the hill on the other side of the ravine.

As we walked, we talked.

I still wanted to call the cops. "It's kidnapping," I said. "Or assault, or something."

"It's kids playing," he said. "No one is going to take us seriously."

"But Cory's missing!"

"Yes. If he were a cute toddler, the cops would swing into action. But he's a teenager, and he's been missing for ten minutes. Cops won't care."

The cell phone rang from inside my pocket. It and my money were the only things I'd taken from the knapsack. "That'll be Mom," I said.

"You want to tell her about Cory?"

"No." I fished out the phone. "Can you imagine, Chris? She'd scream so loud you could hear it from here."

The problem is that my mom can usually tell when I'm lying. I'd have to be very careful. I took a deep breath and opened the phone. Come on, Jules, relax. Be natural.

"Hello there, mother of mine. How's every little thing?"

Too relaxed! Drat. I opened my mouth to correct myself but never got a chance.

"I'm not your mom."

CHAPTER 19 – *Deduction*

For once, the reception was really good. The voice came through clear and precise. I motioned Chris closer and held the phone so we could both hear.

"How'd you get this number?" I asked.

"I got it from your friend Cory. You're Jules, aren't you?"

Sounded like Colin.

"Is Cory all right?"

"Oh, sure. He's fine. *For now.*" Pause. "But you have no idea how scared he's going to be."

In the background a voice saying, "Hurry. It's here."

"Got to go, Jules," said the voice. And the line went dead.

Chris and I stared at each other.

"What do they want?" he asked.

"I don't know. Maybe just to mess us up."

"They're doing that."

I thought about calling back. The phone number was logged under Calls Received. But I didn't know what I'd say after asking them to let Cory go and them saying no.

The top part of the ravine got very steep on this side. Chris strode upward on his stilt legs. I used my hands to hang on to roots and pull myself up. "*The Outdoor Survival*

Handbook says to lean *out* from the slope," he told me. "That way your weight pushes you toward the hill and you grip better. It's vectors, Jules."

"Sure," I said. "Vectors."

"It's not kidnapping," I said. "It's revenge. Cory made fun of Phil, and now they're getting him back."

"Getting us back too."

I nodded. Hurting your friend was a way of hurting you. I thought about Phil making fun of our raft trip. This was a way to make sure we didn't finish it. Yeah, he'd think that was pretty funny.

"I still don't know how they're getting Cory to go along with them," I said. "He runs away from the class on a field trip."

"They must have something for him," said Chris.

We walked along the top of the ravine, past a mesh fence, a wooden fence, and a stone wall. The next back-yard was not fenced. We cut through that one, into the front yard, where a woman was cutting the grass with a power mower. She turned it off to glare at us.

"This is private property. You boys can't keep walking through."

"Sorry," we said, hurrying to the sidewalk. A man raced past us, pushing a stroller on three wheels. The kid in the stroller had her mouth open – wind-tunnel effect, probably. *Whoosh* and they were gone.

"I don't want to get a fence," said the lady with the lawn mower. "But I may have to. I do not like my privacy invaded."

"Sorry," I said again. We were walking away when I got it.

"Wait!" I turned back. "Are you saying that some *other* boys came through here recently, ma'am?"

"I am indeed saying that." She stood with her hands on her hips and her dark eyebrows in a V-shaped depression. "Your friends were here less than ten minutes ago."

Chris punched me.

"Which way did they go?" I asked.

She frowned. "Don't you know? They're your friends."

Oh, dear. Time for some people skills. I forced a smile and walked back.

"You know, ma'am, this is *the* most beautiful lawn I've ever cut across. Incredibly soft underfoot. I know how hard it is to grow grass in Scarborough. The dry summers are scorching."

She didn't start her mower again. I took that for a good sign and kept talking.

"Yes, ma'am. You're doing a wonderful job. I'm sorry for making your job harder. I apologize – not just for me and Chris here, but for my friends who went by earlier." I ducked my head.

It was the right approach. She snorted. "At least I'm *doing* the job. My ex-husband paid a gardener. Now he's gone, and I do my own yard work." She strolled toward us, hands in the pockets of her shorts. Chris, at the approach of another single middle-aged lady, shrank behind me.

"You're amazing, ma'am," I said. "That's what you are. Amazing."

Her eyebrows raised slightly in the middle. Now they looked like the top part of a heart – you know, the shape you use to draw a bird in the distance: ⌒⌒

"When I see our friends, I'll tell them they can't come back this way and walk across your fantastic lawn. Now, there were three of them, right?"

She nodded.

"And you'd recognize Colin since he lives at number seventy-four. This is fifty-seven, so it's just up the street. And they would have headed toward his house."

"Well, they didn't. And I don't know any Colin. They went that way, toward St. Clair." She pointed down at her feet. "See this divot? Do you know how long it takes grass to grow over a divot?"

"Dear, dear. Isn't that awful. I'll certainly tell them that this place is out of bounds." But by the time I'd finished this sentence, Chris was already off and running.

Three winding blocks later, we hit St. Clair. The wealthy subdivision snapped its fingers and disappeared behind us. To our left was a strip mall with a corner store, restaurant, pharmacy, and space for rent. To our right was a strip mall with a donut shop, dollar store, and space for rent. Across six lanes of traffic was a strip mall with an adult video store, a dojo, and a boarded-up, fire-blackened storefront you could rent, I guess, but who'd want to. Suddenly, like twisting a dimmer switch, all the faces around us were a shade darker.

Quick INTERRUPTION Number 3 – Race

I don't want to spend too much time on this. I'm more interested in a story than a social studies essay. But every now and then the issue pops up, like a pimple. Race. Without four hundred years of slavery behind us, racism is not a big deal in Canada – but it's still a deal. I guess it's a deal everywhere. I live in a multiracial suburb in a multiracial city, but the rich neighborhoods are whiter than the poor ones. Subways are mostly a non-white form of transport, and limousines mostly aren't. There's an area of Scarborough called Agincourt – except some people pronounce it *Asian-court* because a lot of the families there are Asian.

All this seems off to me. Without a lot of bad language or meanness, something's wrong. I don't think about being white very often. I wonder how often I'd think about being black. The only time I ever asked Chris about it, he shook his head. You don't know anything about it, Jules, he said.

We were in his dad's car at the time, parked at the side of the highway. His dad had been stopped by the police for driving too fast – though he was going a lot slower than my dad usually drives.

Oh, Chris is black. Handsome, smart, athletic, competitive, utterly trustworthy, not much of a talker, and my best friend, and black. I thought about telling you before, but I didn't want to seem racist. Now it's like I've been saving it up to surprise you, which is racist too, because would I have saved the fact that he was white? Crap. You can go crazy with this stuff. Like I said, I'm happier with the story.

CHAPTER 20 – *Small children must not read this*

"Nice job," said Chris. "You charmed that lady all right. Too bad seventy-four wasn't on her street."

"Or this one." I'd already checked the numbers on St. Clair. We were into the thousands here. "We could be so close!" I said. "They might be a block away!"

"Yeah."

Scarborough streets are wide and well used. Saturday-afternoon traffic meant vans full of kids, trucks full of building supplies. A steady stream of hot, moving metal.

"What if the Preacher got it wrong, Jules?"

"You mean, like, it was another number, not seventy-four?"

"Or maybe it wasn't a number at all. Guy's not exactly Stephen Hawking."

We were both craning around, looking out for three white youths.

"Yeah. But if we don't trust him, then there's nothing for us to do. If we believe him, then we can follow up the clue. And, Stephen Hawking or not, he did remember the joke right."

Chris wiped his face with the bottom of his T-shirt. The ten percent chance of showers was over, and we were back to blue sky. The good thing about being away from the ravine was no bugs. But it was way hotter up here. The pavement shimmered in the windless baking heat. My shoulders and back ran with sweat.

A police car turned into the strip mall on our right and parked in front of the dollar store. A tough-looking officer got out, took off her hat, and wiped her forehead on her sleeve.

I ran over, calling, "Excuse me?"

Down came the arm. Eyes flashed toward me. "Yeah?"

She faced me square on. There were sweat stains on her collar and under her arms.

"Um, I'm worried about a friend of mine. I think he's been kidnapped."

"Kidnapped."

"There's a kind of gang, and I think they took him away about an hour ago. I have the cell phone number they're using and everything."

She moved her mouth around, like she was getting ready to spit. Then she took out her pad, ripped out a piece of paper, and gave it to me, together with a pen.

"I'm going to give you a number," she said. "Write it down and call it. It's my work number. My staff will help you with your kidnapped friend."

I nodded.

"Okay. Write this down. Nine."

She waited while I wrote.

"One," she said. I wrote it.

"One." Oh, okay. I see.

"Got that now? Good. Call the number, and tell them just what you told me." All the time she was talking she was staring me right in the eye. She took the pen back from me and headed into the dollar store. I rejoined Chris near the curb.

"Well?" he said. "Did the cops help?"

"Shut up."

I sprinkled ripped bits of paper over the trash in the gutter, like salt on fries.

"Hey! Hey, look!"

I followed Chris's pointing finger.

"Yes, it's a bus. Very good, Chris. B-u-s. There's another one coming the other way. See it? That's two buses. Can you see any more buses in this picture?"

"Idiot! Look at the number!" He ran toward the bus stop, pulling a transit pass from his pocket.

The westbound bus was a Number 74. (You may have seen this coming, but I didn't. I'm used to taking the LRT.) But, of course, the other bus – eastbound – was a 74 too. Chris realized it at the same time I did. He stopped dead.

I thought about the lady at the westbound bus stop, cigarette in hand . . . the empty eastbound bus . . . Mrs. Private Lawn's recollections . . .

"Cross the street!" I called. "We're going east."

Definite people get their way. Chris nodded without question.

And we went to the corner, pressed the WALK button, and waited patiently for the light to change, the way Officer Friendly taught us in kindergarten. When the light changed to green, and the WALK sign was lit up, we knew we could cross safely. We looked both ways before stepping onto the road, and made sure to walk, not run. Crossing Safely Is the Smart Way!

Ha ha. Not really. We ran like snot across six lanes of traffic, arriving at the vacant stop about four seconds before the eastbound bus.

"You boys are crazy," growled the driver as we climbed on. "Going to get yourselves killed."

Chris used his transit pass and I paid cash. We sat near the back, him calmly, me puffing.

"Why eastbound, Jules?"

So I gave him the computer printout from my mind. "Cory and the Bonesaw boys were only a few minutes ahead of us. Westbound bus stop was crowded. One woman had nearly finished her cigarette, which means she'd been there five or ten minutes. The eastbound stop was empty – and so was this bus. I figured another one had been by recently. It's a few minutes ahead of us now, and our boys are on it."

He smiled. "Sherlock Karapoloff."

"Hey, I call myself that sometimes."

"I know."

"Uh huh." I felt pretty good, considering I was sweating like a river. I stared out the window as my breathing slowed.

"So, what now?"

He had a point. The Number 74 bus would go along St. Clair until it ran into the lake, I guess. When should we get off?

"Well, yes. That's where the, ah, Sherlock thing kind of breaks down." I shrugged. "I suggest we keep our eyes open."

Three stops. Four. We ate up the long Scarborough car-hungry blocks. The place is built for engines, not legs. On our left we passed strip malls and auto dealers and sad motels with letters missing from the sign. VAC-N-Y. On our right I saw trees and the backs of houses. Streets had names like Sunnypoint and Bluffview. The lake was getting closer, the shoreline curving up to meet the road.

A woman with shopping bags stood, even though there were plenty of seats. A man lay across the back seat and fell asleep. Three little kids had enormous fun climbing over the seats while their dad stood in the aisle and caught whoever was about to fall. I must have had a smile on my face, because Dad gave me a wink on their way out at the next stop.

I got a sense of déjà vu. The traffic was a stream, and we were drifting, being carried along from bend to bend, stop to stop. Oh, how I wished we were back on the raft, the three of us, with nothing more dangerous or exciting to worry about than going aground, or maybe picking up a leech.

Six, seven stops. I wondered if we'd gone too far, and how we'd know.

A woman with a shoulder bag plumped herself on the seat in front of Chris. She had wild hair and a dress that looked like it was made of tree bark. She started to go through her bag, cataloguing its contents. As she sorted, she sang.

Chris and I stared across the aisle at each other. The stench coming from her bag was abominable.

"Parsely, sage, rosemary, and asafetida." She cackled and went on. "Remember me to whoever the hell lives there."

Chris moved across to sit near me.

The cell phone rang. Him.

"How are you feeling, *Jules*? Are you worried about your friend?"

I sat up straight.

"Why? What have you done to him?"

The bus was rolling smoothly. Chris stared out the right-side window, his nose wrinkled against the parsley, sage, and asafetida.

"Nothing, yet, Jules. I could tell you different, and you'd have to believe me. I could tell you we were torturing him – sitting on him, pushing him around, kicking him like a football. That'd bother you, wouldn't it?"

"Why are you doing this?"

"He laughed at us. No one laughs at us."

The voice was deadly earnest. It was hard to believe. I wondered what they had planned for Cory. How could you pay someone back for laughing at you?

"What about an apology?"

"Oh, it's too late for apologies, *Jules*. And the best part of it is . . ."

"Is what?"

"Made you ask, didn't I? Ha ha. I like making you do things. The best part is that he doesn't know what we're up to. He thinks we're taking him to his heart's desire. The thing he wants to do most in the world. He thinks we're his friends." He raised his voice. "Hey, Cory? I got Jules on the phone here. You want to talk to him?"

"Jules, you'll never guess what's going on. It is so cool. These guys –"

"Cory! Wait. Where are you?"

"I don't know. We just got off a bus. Now we're waiting for another one."

"Are you all right?"

"Sure. This is fun! I'm so glad I ran into Colin down by the raft. But would you believe it, I lost my cap! They were pushing me around and it fell off."

"Damn it, Cory, where are you? Tell me a name you can see."

I felt like I was talking to a toddler on a cliff. Great danger, limited time, and I had to stay calm.

"Uh . . . McDonald's."

"Cory, that name doesn't help. Give me a street name. And get away from those guys. They're going to hurt you."

"No, Jules. We were wrong about them. They're taking me zombie hunting. Zombie hunting, Jules! Is that cool or what? We're picking up Bonesaw now, and then we're off to kill one hundred and forty-seven zombies." He was so excited, the words were spilling out. "Which reminds me. What is the undead's favorite instrument?"

"They want to hurt you, Cory. They're lying to you."

But he wasn't listening. "Give up? The *zombone*. Get it? *Zombone*."

"Don't you care about our trip, Cory? The raft? Floating downstream to the lake?"

"Sure. But this is zombies! Hang on. Colin wants his phone back."

"Quick!" I shouted. The edge of the cliff was crumbling. "Give me another name. We're looking for you. Give us something. What's the number of your bus?"

We rolled past Midland Avenue, a major intersection. Chris, staring out the right-side window, grabbed my arm so hard it hurt. Three kids waited at the corner for a northbound bus. Two of them wore baseball jackets. The third was Cory, cell phone to his ear, pointing at us as we rolled past.

"There's a bus," he said. "Number 74. We were already on that one."

One of the others – Colin, I guessed – grabbed Cory and turned him around. A northbound bus was pulling into the stop.

"Oh, *here's* our bus now. Bye, Jules," said Cory in my ear.

We'd found them. It was the right intersection all right. I could even see the McDonald's. Chris and I ran to the front of the bus and begged the driver to let us off, but he made us wait to the next stop. "Crazy boys," he said.

CHAPTER 21 – *More complications*

We were too late. I heard the growl of the north-bound bus engine as I got off ours. By the time we ran back to Midland, the bus stop was empty, and the bus itself was disappearing into northbound traffic, an elephant running with a herd of smaller animals.

Chris swore.

"Why won't he run away?" he said.

"He thinks they're his friends," I said. "They bribed him. Bribed him with zombies. He doesn't know they plan to do something awful to him."

Chris wanted to hitchhike after them. "Do something now," he said. "They're farther away every second."

I knew how dangerous hitchhiking was supposed to be. *OMIGOD, Jules,* my mom said. *It's asking for trouble. Do you know how many weirdos are out there?* And *they're looking for you, all of them, constantly on the lookout for kids to prey on!* Personally, I'd say it's a brave driver who picks up two thirteen-year-old boys. Anyway, I agreed to try it, and we put out our thumbs and nothing happened. No driver even looked at us. We were still standing there five minutes later when a school bus stopped for the red light and two teenagers jumped out the back, landing right at our feet.

"Shh!" said the white kid. Yes, one of them was

black and one was white. They were dressed in shorts and T-shirts.

The black kid grinned. "You guys want a lift?" The cargo door at the back of the school bus flapped open. He and his partner took off down the street.

Ten seconds later we were sitting at the back of the bus, heading north, wearing fluorescent orange vests that we'd found on the floor. The kid next to us wore a vest too. I figured we should try to blend in.

"Don't tell," I whispered.

The kid leaned against the back of the seat with his eyes closed.

"Nothing to tell," he said. "Didn't see anything."

"Great. So, where are we going?" I asked. "Some kind of camp?"

"Yeah. That's right." He gave a tight smile.

Only eight or ten kids on the bus. They slept or gazed off into space. No one cared about us. They all wore the vests. The counselor stood up at the front, next to the bus driver.

"This is a crazy idea," I said to Chris.

He didn't say I was wrong. But he explained to make me look wrong. "If we want to catch up to Cory, we have to go faster than Cory, right?"

"Uh, right," I said.

"*Are* we going faster than Cory?"

He pointed ahead. The light turned green as we got there, and we pulled past a city bus. I checked – it was empty. Not Cory's.

"Uh, I guess so."

"So, is this really a crazy idea, Jules?"

"Yes!" I said right away. "Yes yes yes. We could be found out any time and kicked off. Cory could get off his bus. It's an insane . . . " My voice trailed off.

We were catching up to another city bus. This one seemed to be full of people. And the advertisement on the back – a local radio show – was the one I'd seen on Cory's bus.

"Sit down. Shut up." The guy next to us barely moved his lips to speak, his voice creeping out like a cat burglar. "Don't give Vinegar a reason to yell."

"Vinegar?"

He gave an almost imperceptible nod toward the front of the bus. He still hadn't opened his eyes. "Vinegar yells all the time. Anyone steps out of line, he yells."

"Gee, this does sound like camp," I said.

We rolled up beside the radio-show bus at the next intersection. Chris peered through the window, cupping his hands against the glare. "I can see them!" he cried. "There's Cory."

I got out the cell phone, found the last caller's number, and phoned it.

Chris stayed at the window. "The call-in guy is on the phone. It's him."

I smiled. Time for a little revenge.

"Hi, Colin," I said. "It's me, Jules. Enjoying your bus ride?"

Silence. Let him worry a bit.

"You know those horror movies where the babysitter finds out the mysterious phone calls are coming from inside the house? Do you, Colin? Well, I'm calling from inside the bus."

"We're not on a bus anymore."

"Yes you are, Colin. You're on Midland Avenue on a dirty 135 bus waiting for the light to change three blocks north of Elgin. You've got the cell phone against your . . ." I covered the mouthpiece. "Which ear, Chris?" He pointed. I uncovered. "Your right ear."

I heard a startled yelp, and the connection went dead. I smiled for the first time in hours.

"*What* is that?"

Standing in front of me was Vinegar: six feet of lean and mean. His voice bit like acid – I can see how he got his nickname. He pointed at the cell phone with a claw-like finger. I closed it.

"*Is* that a cell phone?"

He talked like an army sergeant. Reminded me more than ever of my day camp. Except that my counselors were all teenagers, and Old Vinegar was, well, old.

"*Is* that a cell phone?"

I could have made a smart answer. *No, it's an ostrich*, I could have said. *No, it's a bagel. No, it's the Treaty of Versailles.* But I felt that this was not the time.

His hand flashed out and grabbed the phone from me.

"Hey! That's mine."

The bus came awake. The campers looked back at me. No expression on any of the faces, but you could tell they were interested.

"You can't –" I began. But he could. He put the phone in his pocket. When I stood up, he pushed me down. Hard.

"*You* know the rules." His eyes were small and deep set, so that he looked like he was peering at me from inside a cave of bone and flesh. An intimidating face. An intimidating guy.

The bus started up, and the rear door opened an inch or two and banged shut.

"*What* is that? *Is* that an open door?"

Once again the ostrich remark would have been wrong.

He pushed me out of the way, slammed the door shut, and locked it with a padlock that was attached to the inside of the door. He ran his eyes around the bus, counting bodies.

"Seven and two." He nodded in satisfaction. "No one missing."

We pulled into the right lane, ahead of the city bus. Over the next hill was a power cut – a belt of public land wider than a football field where ten-story pylons stood like a bucket brigade of giants, passing electricity from terminal to terminal. Our bus turned off the main road into the power cut. The city bus, with Cory inside, continued north.

Chris and I stared at each other.

We drove down a grassy hill to a small brick building. Old Vinegar hustled us out and lined us up against the side of the bus. He counted us again. The driver went into the building and came out with garbage bags and pointed sticks.

This was not a camp.

"There's been a mistake," I said to Vinegar. "We shouldn't be here."

This was a community service detail. Chris and I had sneaked onto a bus full of convicts who were repaying their debt to society by picking up garbage.

"A mistake!" I said again. "Two other guys jumped off the bus. They should be here, not us. We're not criminals – only idiots."

"Shut up!" said Vinegar.

I took my stick and bag.

"You remember them, don't you?" I said to the guy who'd been beside us. "Tell him. Tell him!"

He gave his small, tucked-in smile.

"Nothing to tell," he said. "Didn't see anything."

CHAPTER 22 – *Frustrating*

I can't remember ever spending such an awful afternoon. It was hot, tiring, boring, and frustrating – a lot of each one of these. The giant power pylons hummed constantly. The sun hit like a hammer. When I swallowed, the inside of my throat felt like sandpaper. The trash was literally neverending. It became an element to me: I breathed it, wore it, moved through it. And every minute I worked, every candy wrapper I picked up, I knew that Cory was getting farther and farther away.

Chris felt as bad as I did. "Thanks," he said, around four o'clock, as we dumped our full bags and picked up new ones.

"What for?"

"For not saying *I told you so*. The bus was my idea."

"Stop it," I said. "I went along. And it was a good idea. It almost worked. Really, it was me and my cell phone that got us in trouble. You should be mad at me."

"Yeah," he said.

"If it weren't for me, we'd have caught up to Cory by now."

"Yeah. Damn you, Jules."

"Yeah. Damn me."

We smiled at each other.

"Thing is, we have to think of something else. Don't regret your old idea, Chris. Get a new one."

A work gang of grown-ups joined ours. One of the men was familiar. Took me a moment to place him. Old Vinegar counted everyone up. "Sixteen and three," he said. The other supervisor nodded.

"What's that about?" I asked Chris. "Seven and two. Sixteen and three."

"Man's keeping track of us, Jules," said Chris. "He wants to know how many white, how many black."

I checked quickly. There were three white guys, counting me. One was a kid from our bus. The other was the familiar man. Everyone else was darker colored.

"Ew," I said. On a bunch of levels.

Candy wrappers. There were other kinds of garbage, of course – newspapers and magazines, cardboard boxes, Styrofoam containers for coffee or hamburgers, fliers advertising everything from cauliflower to contentment – but there were more candy wrappers than anything else. I had no idea that our civilization had such sweet teeth.

To keep from going insane, I tried counting the different kinds, keeping a running total. Which was the most popular? So far it was a dead heat between Snickers and Skor, with M&Ms close behind. All good choices, as far as I was concerned. I was getting hungry.

I tried not to think about time passing, or Cory moving out of our reach, or how on earth we were going to get out of this. Or what our parents were going to say.

I asked Chris if he'd had any new ideas. He shook his head.

"Me neither," I said. "Let's keep our eyes and ears open."

He straightened up with a frown. "And noses."

Roscoe, the hobo, had moved into range.

He was the one I'd recognized in the new busload. There was no mistaking the wide shoulders under the army jacket or the ham-sized hands sticking out of it. Or the smell. He knew us too. He gripped his sharp stick like a harpoon and moved threateningly in our direction.

Last time we'd seen him, he accused Chris of beating him up. *You're the guy*, he'd said.

That's what this afternoon needed to make it perfect. Fear.

Vinegar led a group of us across the road to pick trash on the other side, and Roscoe followed. But the closer he came to us, the slower he moved. Now that he was right beside us, Roscoe was shaking his head in plain bewilderment.

"You're *not* the guy," he growled at Chris. "I thought you were. But you're not."

The smell coming off him was strong and sharp – Dumpster with a hint of gasoline.

"You didn't hurt me, that time, down by the Rep House."

"No," said Chris.

"You're black." He stared at me. "Your friend is black."

"Yes," I said.

"But he looks like the white kid who kicked me. Strange, you know."

All the threat was out of Roscoe. Unless he was going to breathe on us, we were safe. He speared a cardboard container of fries and checked it to see if there were any left inside before putting it in his garbage bag. Yeck.

Chris moved off. Roscoe called after him. "Sorry, kid!"

Then he leaned toward me. "What did they get you for? I was D&D sometime last week. You know, drunk and disorderly. What about you guys?"

"Oh, we don't belong here," I said. "We're innocent."

"Sure." He belched. "Sure."

I'd been kidding about him killing us by breathing out, but it was pretty grim there for a second. *Vlad the Exhaler.* I hurried after Chris, trying to remember where I'd heard about the Rep House.

Ten minutes, a hundred wrappers, a thousand dry swallows later, I heard a voice speak to me from out of the earth.

"What a loser!" it said.

I wondered if I was hearing things. Hallucinations could be aural as well as visual.

"Yeah! Spending the afternoon picking up garbage," said another voice.

"Loser for sure," said the first voice.

They might have been hallucinations, at that. I mean, hallucinations come from inside your mind, right? And this was how I felt about myself. *Loser for sure.* But when I walked a few paces forward, I came to a metal trap door anchored in concrete. A storm sewer. And the voices were coming from inside. I peered through the grating and saw two faces hanging in space, four eyes gleaming in the darkness of the shaft.

"Hi, guys," I said.

"Hi, loser," said the first voice, which came from a black kid with a round face and oversized teeth. "Hey, Marty, look at the loser." I might not have told you he was black, except that the other kid – Marty – was white, with a long face and little red-rimmed eyes.

He laughed, showing small, curiously pointy teeth.

So, no hallucinations. I was being spied on by two bored kids, about my age, with nothing to do this Saturday afternoon but hang around and bug people.

I heard a knock on the front door of my brain. I went to answer it, and there was the FedEx guy. He handed me a package marked IDEA – Fragile.

These two guys might be our ticket out of here. It'd take some work, but it was worth trying. I looked around carefully. Chris and I were pretty much alone in this part of the garbage-strewn field. Roscoe was a stone's throw away, eating something he'd found. Vinegar was back by the road. Okay, then.

"Loser, huh?" I said out loud. I smiled as wide as I could. "I'd say *you* guys are the losers."

Chris heard me and looked over. I made a shushing gesture.

"What?" said the first kid. "Look who's talking."

I worked my way over to the sewer and saw the two faces more clearly. They were pressed close to the underside of the grating.

"What'd you mean, calling me and Vince losers?" asked the other kid. Marty.

I smiled down at them. "I'm having fun in the sun, boys. You're hanging around in a dark sewer. Mold in there, I bet. And rats. And you. Perfect. You two are the losers, if you ask me."

"Shut up. It's cool in here. We can be home in two minutes. And we aren't criminals."

"Course you're not," I said with as much sneer as I could find.

I stabbed sharply into the ground beside the grating with my pointed stick. Held it and pulled out. "Hah! Got him!" I cried.

I wiggled the stick a little.

"What is it?" asked Vince. "Can you see, Marty?"

"No."

I stuffed the stick and its contents into my sack and carried on.

"You two aren't criminals," I said. "You're too scared to commit a crime. You wouldn't hurt a fly. You sure wouldn't stab a mouse with a stick like this." I held it up. "Would you?"

Silence, except for the power lines humming overhead.

"Was that what that was just now? Was it a mouse?" asked Marty excitedly. I sympathized. There's something about poking things with a stick that goes to the heart of you. A basic boy instinct.

I could have lied and said, *Yep, third one today.* I could have told the truth and said, *Nope, an apple core.* I decided to ignore the question. Let Marty use his imagination. His imagination was my ally.

"Why, my partner and I put a man in hospital," I said.

More silence. Then, together, like a chorus, "You did?"

"Truth."

(It was truth too. We went with my mom when she drove Dad to St. Mike's. He'd eaten two plates of hot peppers and was convinced that he was going to explode.)

I had the guys set up. Now it was time for the knockout. I poked up an empty potato chip bag (sweet chili heat – my favorite) and a yellow box that had at one point held twenty Timbits. And paused dramatically.

"Heyyy," I said, just like The Fonz. "Would you look at . . . *that!*" I bent down near the grate. "Whoa!"

"What is it?" whispered Marty, the white kid.

"Hey, Chris!" I called. "Get a look at this." I held up a magazine.

"Is it porn?" asked Marty.

What a mind he had. Of course it was what I was hoping he'd say. Another basic instinct. I didn't answer.

"Is it?"

I went over to Chris, showed him the magazine. (It

was last month's *Better Kitchens and Bathrooms*.) We put our heads together and stared down at one of the photo spreads.

"Wow," I said. "Have you ever seen them that big?"

He shook his head. "Never."

"*What* are you guys talking about?" said Marty. "What are that big?"

"What do you think, Marty?" I said. (Well, what do *you* think? Towels, if you must know. Great big honking bath towels with roses on them.)

"And soft! Don't they look soft, Chris?" I said.

"Soft, all right."

"And so touchable! Don't you want to touch them?"

"Oh, I do," said Chris. His mouth twitched.

"Me too. Imagine how they'd feel against your cheek. Oh, my. Oh, my. You could just . . . lose yourself . . . in them for . . . weeks!"

"Jules?"

"Huh?" I opened my eyes. "Oh, right. Thanks, Chris."

I had to be careful. Imagination is a tricky thing. These were just towels.

"Can we see?" Marty rattled the bars of the grate. "Please! Vince and I want to see!"

"Well, I don't know. Can you guys climb out of that sewer?"

"Sure. We do it all the time." He started to lift up the grate from below.

"Wait!"

I whipped my head around. Sighed. "There's a guard over there. You don't have the orange vest. He'll notice."

"Aw. Let us borrow –"

"Sorry, guys." I put the magazine under my arm and went back to work. Chris raised his eyebrows at me. I held up my hand, palm out. Wait. He nodded.

The sewer grate was at the bottom of a little rise. I started up, poking as I went, but stayed within earshot. A minute later Marty's voice came, plaintively.

"You still there?"

I went back to the sewer grate. "What is it?"

"Can we see the porn magazine?"

"This?" I opened it at random, then shut it quick. "Ew! – Gross!"

I took another peek. Shuddered. "Oh, wow!"

"What? What?" They practically squeaked with excitement.

I put the magazine in my trash bag. "That picture is too weird for me. Listen, I'm going to try another section of the power cut. Bye, guys."

"Oh, come on. Let us see. *Please* let us see!"

I sighed, looked around, bent down.

"Okay," I whispered. "Here's the deal . . ."

There were thirteen metal steps set into the concrete wall of the storm sewer. The sewer pipe ran at a slight downward angle. So did Chris and I – the pipe wasn't as tall as we were. There was daylight at the end. We hurried toward it while Marty and Vince were putting on orange

vests and pawing through the garbage bag for porn.
Marty was chubby and brown-haired, and Vince was tall.
From a distance they'd pass for us.

"What'll Vinegar say when he realizes we've gone?"
I asked.

Chris considered.

"I think he'll count everyone up and say, Sixteen
and three."

I had to agree.

Should I have worried about Vince and Marty? I
didn't. They'd call their parents from wherever the bus let
them off. They'd hate us for suckering them with *Better
Kitchens and Bathrooms*, but they'd never tell anyone
about it.

And really, it served them right for having such wild
and twisted imaginations.

I could live with it.

CHAPTER 23 – *Food and quarters*

Chris was laughing. I could hear him, chuckling quietly in the dimness as we made our way down the pipe.

"What's so funny?" I said.

"You are."

There was light up ahead. We hurried. The pipe was dry, and our footsteps made soft squinching sounds, like new shoes on a clean floor.

"Me?"

"Yeah, you. We've been friends since kindergarten, Jules. Always the same way. You were the talker, and I was the doer. I always figured I came off better. I solved the problem, you made the joke . . . I was happier being me. But after today, I don't know. I'm going to start looking to you for answers when the spit hits the fan. I don't back down, but sooner or later I run out of ideas and start hitting people. You . . . you never quit. You keep talking. And that's why we're here."

"In a sewer," I said, smiling. "Without our friend, and with no idea how to find him. Lost and tired, and in the dark. That's where we are."

The light was getting brighter. We were almost out of the sewer.

"Don't be like that. We escaped from a chain gang! You talked us out of a Ministry of Corrections work detail.

That's like bluffing your way out of a POW camp. Jules, you got the gift, man. I used to think I could boss you around, but I see now it was always the other way. You're the pitcher, man. I'm the catcher. With you on it, we'll find Cory. We'll finish this trip."

This was probably as much as I'd ever heard Chris say at one time before.

I wanted to tell him something nice too, but the only things I could think of sounded kind of wrong, so I just said, "Thanks."

"I'm so hungry," said Chris.

"I wish you had not reminded me of that."

"Why?"

"Because I was just thinking to myself that I should call home, but now I am overwhelmed with a picture of grilled meat on a bun, and I have to do something about it. We'll find a restaurant, put all our money on the counter, and buy what we can."

We hopped out of the storm sewer into a ravine like the one at home. The creek was narrower than ours, and the trees smaller, but everything felt familiar. Like our ravine, this one was a nod back in time. Looking downstream, you could believe it was a thousand years ago. It would not have been wrong to see a group of Ojibwa women on the rocks, pounding away at the washing.

Chris squinted up at the sky. "This creek flows the same way ours does. I bet they join together."

"I bet they always did. Long before any power cuts or bungalows."

"Or candy wrappers."

We hopped across the creek and into the woods on the other side and were immediately shot dead by a Martian.

So much for historical perspective.

He was about five years old, with a space suit made of garbage bags and a football helmet and gloves that were too big for him. A ruthless kid, he jumped at us from behind a clump of alders and commenced firing. No warning at all.

The gun flashed and made noise. Pretty good, really. I clutched my heart and fell backward.

"Oh," said the kid. "I thought you were Marty and Vince."

"You got me anyway. Good shooting." I staggered convincingly.

"Did I really get you?" Suddenly serious.

"Oh yeah."

"Then stop moving. This Martian pistol fires a paralyzing ray."

"Oh," I said.

"You can't talk either," he said.

Chris leaned against a tree with a half smile on his face.

"Not much of a game, is it?" I said. "You shoot me, I freeze and shut up. What happens now? I can't come with you, and I can't fight you. If I can't even open my mouth, what's the point?"

"You're still talking!" he said. "Stop talking!"

"Kid," said Chris, shaking his head, "you have *no* idea."

The kid tried to fire another shot, but his gloved finger got jammed in the trigger so the gun wouldn't fire. We left him. Halfway up the hill we found another little kid. He wore a cape and a mask, and he was standing still and silent.

Paralyzed.

The top of the hill was a vacant lot in the middle of a new subdivision. The setting sun angled right at our faces. We walked along a street full of sparkling bungalows, green sod, new bikes. It was a million degrees.

"Yes, it's been a big day," I said. "Our journey's in tatters and we don't know how to get back on track. But first things first."

"Food."

"Fried food," I elaborated.

We picked the first chain restaurant we found, went to the bathroom to wash the garbage off our hands, pooled our money, and ordered burgers and fries and shakes and pies. There was exactly seventy-five cents left. Enough for three phone calls.

We decided to tell our parents the truth. We had learned our lesson, and we knew now that lying is wrong, and lying to your parents is doubly wrong. Wrong wrong.

Kidding again. We decided to do a double switch. Chris didn't want to – he really does hate lying to his parents – but in the end I convinced him.

We couldn't tell our parents the truth – not with Cory still out there. They would never trust us again. I'd be twenty before my mom would let me cross the street by myself. And what could we tell Cory's mom? So we'd tell Chris's folks that *mine* would make the pickup and bring Chris back to my place for a sleepover, and meanwhile tell my parents that I'd be sleeping over at Chris's place. That way we could stay out late by ourselves, and no parents would worry.

First part worked like a charm. Chris's dad was happy not to have to drive all the way down to the lake. "Glad you're enjoying yourself, son," he said. (He was that kind of dad. I don't think my dad has ever called me son. Usually, I'm *Hey!*) "Too bad about the cell phone, but you're okay." We'd agreed to say that the cell phone was lost. Chris didn't want his parents to think he'd be phoning when he wouldn't be. And we didn't want anyone phoning Old Vinegar.

I called Cory's place next. A little girl answered the phone with a giggle. No daycare on Saturday. This was one of his sisters. When I asked to speak to her mom, she said no and hung up.

My turn now, with our last quarter, and wouldn't you know it: I lost our money. I punched the number, the coin dropped, and then the line went dead.

I punched the coin return.

"What happened?" asked Chris.

"I don't know. I lost the quarter."

No more money. "I'll make it a collect call," I said. "After we eat."

CHAPTER 24 – *Failure to communicate*

A fast-food restaurant is a treat. The canned music, the antiseptic smells, the bathrooms down the hall – it's all unreal and yet comforting, just like the warm, salty, fatty food. It's coming in out of a cold day, flopping into a chair, and letting the feeling come back to your hands, realizing that you don't have to move for a while. It's time out.

Chris and I ate, and smiled, and talked about what we'd do with a million dollars, and put our horrible afternoon on hold.

"Would you buy a private jet?" I asked.

"And fly it. What about you?"

"I'm trying to figure out how many cashews I could fit into one room."

We talked about what we'd do if zombies attacked the restaurant, but the conversation reminded us of Cory and we fell silent.

"Where are they taking him, Jules?"

"I dunno. To see Bonesaw, but I don't know where that is."

"Think, Jules. Think."

"Yeah, well, you think too. I don't want it all hanging on me."

I was finished my fries, but Chris wasn't. I stole a couple. I was going over my phone conversation with

Cory. He thought they were taking him to see zombies.

"What do you think of when you hear the word *zombie*?" I said.

Chris shrugged. "Undead."

"Keep going."

"Evil dead. Dawn of the dead. Rotting corpses. Brain-eating . . . voodoo."

"Voodoo?"

"Isn't that how you make zombies? Remember that show about the voodoo queen who could raise the dead to become her slaves?"

"Oh yeah." She had a French accent and scary eyes, and she slithered when she danced.

Hmm.

How to find out more about Bonesaw? All I knew was that he was huge – over six feet. *A big boy*, the cop had called him.

Hmm.

I wondered if Jasmine would know. Or Miriam.

Hmm.

"What is it, Jules?"

"Nothing. Let me make my phone call."

The operator had one of those nasal voices. "Tha-ank you, sir," she said. "I'm calling the number for you now."

"Allo?" said the voice from my house. Not Mom or Dad's – Baba's voice.

Oh, oh.

The operator went into her spiel. "I have a collect call from . . . Jules."

"Jules?" said Baba. "Jules not home. Jules on boat ride. His mama and papa gone to movies. I only at home. No one wants to talk to me."

"Do you accept –"

"Is not my house. I live in the basement but is not my home. After big storm, I am topless."

"Will you accept the collect call from Jules?"

"I tell you already. Jules not home all day. I take message."

"Baba!" I called into the phone. "It's me."

The operator began again, but Baba interrupted.

"Jules! I hear you. Where are you? You are with this telephone lady? Where is your little phone?"

"Say yes, Baba. Say you'll accept the call. Then we can talk."

"I call back. Where are you with this lady? Is number in phone book?"

"No, this is a collect call. I need you to say you accept the call."

Even a simple *yes* would have done. But Baba didn't say *yes*.

"Polka dots," she said. "Jules, you like polka dots? I was downtown today, looking for birthday shirt –"

The operator was a real trier. She broke in firmly.

"Ma'am, do you accept a call from –"

"Jules – not – home," said Baba, louder and slower. "Why you not understand, lady? And what size you are, Jules? Medium?"

"Baba –"

"I get medium, okay?"

"Do you accept –"

"Vrashka rabota!" said Baba and hung up. After a moment, I did too.

"Did you explain things?" asked Chris.

"Yes, and no."

"Want to try again?"

"No."

One thing Baba said made sense, though. *Phone book.* I swung the directory out from under the pay phone, checked the Yellow Pages and then the business Whites. I tried under R, the first part of the name, and found dozens of places to get repairs, reprints, and reproductions. Nowhere to eat. Just to make sure, I tried H (hey, for years the Royal Ontario Museum was listed under T for The) and found a whole page of stores and services (two of them you had to be eighteen years old to call!), including three restaurants – none of which was the right one.

Damn.

"What are you looking for?" asked Chris. I told him. "Roscoe mentioned the place," I said. "And so did Walter."

"Oh, yeah." Chris nodded casually. "So, uh, what now?"

"I don't know."

"Come on, Jules. Think of something."

INTERRUPTION – I guess this is Number 4. Maybe the last one.

Here's the list of businesses from the telephone directory. No choir sang when I came to the key one, but I remembered it a half hour later, on the bus. That's when I hit the lady on the leg.

House About Them Apples!	
House by You?	restaurant
House Everything?	realtor
House My Driving?	personal shoppers
House of Attitudes	long-distance transport
House of Flags	hair salon
House of Furniture	paving stones
House of Pancakes	warehouse
House of Pain	restaurant
House Stupid Do You Think I Am?	dungeon*
House the Boss?	marriage counselor
House to House Search	headhunter
House Tomorrow, Then?	realtor
House, The Charm	meeting arranger
House, The Corner	jewelry store
House, The Reptile	restaurant
House Tricks	natural history museum
House Wheat It Is!	escort agency*
House Your Day Been?	bakery
House Your Father?	therapist
	adoption service

*18+

(In case you were wondering, *Vrashka rabota* is Macedonian for "devil's work." My baba uses the phrase to describe all machinery.)

CHAPTER 24 – *Back again*

One of my sister's favorite musicians is a piano player named Ben Folds. We listen to him in the car when she's driving, and some of his lyrics stick in my head. He has one song about a rebel who gets old and becomes respectable. "It's no fun to be the man," he sings, or something like that. And what I'm getting at is that Ben is right. It's tough to be the one with the answers. Imagine being a general, or the president of a country. Everyone looking to you to save the day. I had one guy looking to me, and I didn't like it.

I realized, meeting Chris's clear gaze across the ketchup-stained table, that in all the contests and confrontations that he and I had been in together, *he* had been the man. The doer, as he put it. It had been up to him to score the goal, to come first, to stand his ground. To win. I'd had the easy job – looking on, applauding, making a joke.

"Come on, Jules," said Chris. "Think of something."

I wonder if he felt relieved not to be the man, for once.

When you don't know what to do, try making an assumption and see where it takes you. I assumed they were taking Cory to Bonesaw. I didn't know anything about him except that he was big and scary and staying at Phil's house, and I didn't know Phil's address or phone number. But I knew someone who did.

"Let's go back to Jasmine's," I said.

"That place!" Uneasily.

"Don't worry, I'll protect you from her mom. Thing is, Jasmine knows everyone. Even Bonesaw. She can answer some questions. And she has a phone we can use."

He nodded doubtfully. "How're we going to get back there?"

"You still got your transit pass, don't you?"

He sighed. "Bus sneak?"

"Bus sneak."

There was a bus stop right in front of the burger place. A crowd of people waited, fidgeting, impatient. Perfect. The bus came over the hill a few minutes later.

"My pass," said Chris. "You go first."

So I boarded in the first crush of passengers, flashing Chris's pass in the driver's face when he was distracted by all the other people crowding on. I ran down the aisle and handed the pass out the window to Chris, waiting on the sidewalk. He sauntered on at the end of the line. The gimmick is foolproof as long as the bus stop is crowded. We got off at St. Clair and did it again for the bus ride back to our ravine.

Return journeys are never as exciting as outgoing – not worth describing, except that it was on this journey that part of the truth came to me.

Chris and I were standing in a packed bus, with our noses pressed up against the window. The bus slowed in front of an unfinished billboard. All you could read was

RAP . . .

    . . . BALL.

It occurred to me that you didn't need the other half of the letters. RAP BALL meant Raptors Basketball.

"What are you staring at, Jules? Raps aren't going to win anything this year."

"I know."

"Hey, I think this is our stop." Chris began to edge his way through the crowd.

I thought about the poster. Rap for Raptors. And saw what I should have seen earlier.

"That's *it*!" I brought my fist down to punch myself in the leg. "Oh, sorry!"

Not my leg, as it turned out. The lady standing beside me wore a short skirt and a long jacket, and smelled nice. I'd hit her leg instead of mine, and now she was rubbing the spot and asking me what the hell I was doing.

"Sorry, sorry. I just got an idea, is all."

"What *kind* of idea?" She frowned deeply and tugged on the sleeve of the guy beside her. "Sam, this little white boy just hit me in the leg."

Sam looked a long way down at me. "You *hit* my Maureen?" His voice sounded like hail on the windshield.

"Um . . ."

"He said he got an idea too."

"You got *ideas* about my Maureen?"

I couldn't see this ending well. "OMIGOD," I said, looking past Sam's shoulder. (For a second I startled myself. I sounded just like my mom.) "Is that a scorpion?"

When he turned round, I dropped to my hands and knees and scrambled through a maze of legs. I managed to steer clear of Sam's size-thirteen zip-up boots, but Maureen got me in the ribs with a pointy toe. *Ouch!* Served me right, I guess.

"Chris, wait up."

We were hurrying back toward the ravine and Jasmine's house. Come to think of it, we were hurrying last time we'd been here. The sun was low in the sky and way north of us. Seemed like I'd been awake since forever. Summer days last so long.

"Chris, I know about the Rep House now."

"The restaurant you were looking for in the phone book? Yeah, I was thinking about it too. You couldn't find the name because the place is closed, right? Didn't Walter say it was closed?"

"No. I couldn't find it because I didn't know the full name. Now I do. It isn't even a restaurant, Chris. There's a restaurant there, but it's a museum."

The gardening lady's house was on our right. We sped up.

"Jules, what's wrong? Why are you holding your side?"

"Some things you can't talk your way out of."

REVELATION

CHAPTER 25 – *No time for titles*

We cut through the house next door to the gardening lady's. The lawn was empty, but the smell of barbecue hung in the air, burnt offerings to the god of mealtime. The fence around the yard did not have a gate in it. We had to climb over. "Imagine having a ravine in your backyard and not using it," said Chris.

"Imagine having a plate of barbecued ribs in front of you."

"Jules, we just ate. You hungry already?"

"Don't have to be hungry to eat."

I followed him down the slope to the creek, but on the way back up the other side I took the lead, and he fell back. We went round by the public easement and up the walk to the front door of Jasmine's house. The police cars were gone, and the neighborhood breathed its usual air of quiet wealth and pride. The high windows of the turret across the road caught the setting sun.

My heart was beating as I rang the bell. (Well, duh. What I mean is, I could feel it beating.) I had, I am pretty sure, a foolish smile on my face. It took a while for Miriam to open the door, and when she did she had a funny smile on her face too.

"Chunky!" she said. "And Chris."

She cleared her throat and straightened her hair, which was mussed.

For a second I forgot why we were there. I was remembering our kiss. She'd changed clothes again, into a light summer dress that set off her caramel skin and white teeth. She smelled of perfume.

"Aren't you guys supposed to be floating down the creek?"

Chris was peering into the house the way I peer into a room with a hornet in it. Looking for Connie, I guessed.

I asked if we could talk to Jasmine. Miriam held on to the door even after we'd come into the hall. As if she was hoping we wouldn't stay long.

"Jasmine is downtown, shopping. The party went so badly that Aunt Connie took her to Holt Renfrew to make up for it."

Chris relaxed visibly.

"So you're alone?" I said.

"Well, no. There's, uh, Valerie, of course. She's upstairs."

Oh, yeah, Valerie. The little sister.

"Of course," I said. "Listen closely, Miriam. Cory is missing, and we think Bonesaw is involved. What can you tell us about him?"

"*Bonesaw*?"

A stranger glided into the hall through the French doors off to the left. "How do these guys know about Bonesaw?" he asked Miriam.

He was older than me, but a lot like me. Casual clothes, glasses. He carried a little extra weight too, like me. He shook his hair out of his eyes. Nineteen? Twenty? About my sister's age. He smelled like Miriam. Her perfume.

"This is Jasmine's brother," said Miriam. "He was working today, so he missed the party. Bunky, meet Jules and Chris."

She'd mentioned his name before. We waved. He said hi.

"Bunky and I were just talking," Miriam said. She closed the front door now.

Why did she tell me that, when I hadn't asked? What did it mean, anyway, *just talking*? I hadn't known Bunky long, but I didn't like him.

"What do you think of Bonesaw, Jules?" he asked. "Impressive, eh?"

"I've never even seen him," I said. "I don't know anything about him, except that he's big and scary. I mean, people scream when they see him. And he likes to go swimming. Phil uses his name to scare people. Is he from around here?" I asked.

"Around here?" Miriam laughed. "Chunky, how well do you know the Scarborough fauna?"

Bunky shook his head. "Bonesaw's from Colombia. I helped Professor Aherne capture him last year."

You ever wake from a deep sleep and feel completely disoriented? For a moment, nothing makes sense. It's not that you don't know where you are – you don't even know *who* you are. It's like you've been cut off from yourself and your own understanding of humanity. There's a thick, dark curtain between you and everything you know. You are sure you are going crazy. That's how I felt now, standing in the darkened hall.

Phrases snuck into my memory.

"Daddy's in South America . . ."

"Gimme my hook . . ."

"Well over six feet . . ."

"Zombies, Jules! They're going to show me . . ."

"Voodoo."

"He's in the pool and I can't get him out by myself . . ."

Then, in your disoriented state, you catch a glimpse of light from a window, or hear a snatch of a childhood song, or smell a familiar smell, and that one contact with your past, with your self, is enough to call you to sanity. The thick, dark curtain falls to the floor in a heap. Suddenly, you know everything.

"Bonesaw is a snake," I said. "Isn't he."

"A *snake*?" Chris was surprised and upset.

"*Boa constrictor imperator*, to be precise," said Bunky. "Fresh from the Colombian jungle. I brought him back three days ago."

"A big boa." I had to laugh at myself. That cop had said it as plain as he could, talking on the radio to the sergeant. *He's a big boa.*

"Not that big," said Bunky. "Two years ago, Professor Aherne and I studied an anaconda well over twenty feet long."

"Bunky works with the professor," said Miriam proudly. "He gets phone calls from South America all the time."

Oh, I didn't like this guy at all.

Chris was shaking his head. "I thought Bonesaw was a kid's nickname. I never saw any snake at the party."

"Yeah." I was thinking back to the scene in the kitchen. "When I heard the screaming, I pictured this big bully scaring everyone out of the pool."

"*What*?" It was Bunky's turn to be upset. "Bonesaw was here? *In the pool!*" He whirled on Miriam, grabbing her with both hands. "Why didn't you tell me?"

"I *did* tell you." She shook herself free. "You weren't listening. I said Phil showed up with Bonesaw and the gang, and the party got out of hand and some neighbor called the cops."

"That idiot!"

Who was he talking about? "Bonesaw?" I asked.

"No, Phil! Bringing Bonesaw here. Doesn't he know anything? Always showing off to his friends. He shouldn't be swimming in chlorinated water."

"Phil?"

"No, Bonesaw! He's delicate and expensive, and missing home. Chlorine's not good for him. He should be in the acclimatizing tank at Professor Aherne's house. That's where I put him when I got back from Bogotá."

Bunky dug a cell phone from a deep pocket in his shorts. "I've got to save him," he muttered, pacing back through the French doors. We followed.

I was pretty sure he meant Bonesaw, this time.

"The pool filter has been on all the time, right, Miriam?"

"Sure, Bunky. What's the problem?"

"No problem. I'll check it later. Bonesaw's been sick, is all. I hope he didn't foul the pool."

Miriam made a face and left the room.

Bunky entered the phone number. "Hello, Daisy?" he said. "It's me, Bunky. How are you, honey? That's great. Listen, could I talk to your brother? No, not Edwin, I mean your big brother. I want to talk to Phil."

The French doors led to a room with couches and shelves and a piano. Could have been a living room or a music room. I was still trying to come to terms with the revelation. How had I not realized that Bonesaw was a reptile? How had I been so blind? If only I'd gone outside at the party and seen him in the pool.

"We should have known about Bonesaw, Chris," I muttered. "We are such idiots. That hook thing – it's for picking up snakes. I've seen them on the Discovery Channel."

"Yeah."

Chris was on the carpet with his hands laced behind his head, doing sit-ups. This heartened me. So much had happened to him today – I was glad to see part of him unchanged.

"I guess Phil must be used to snakes, since his dad catches them and keeps them in the house. But still, you don't expect to meet a big snake at a pool party."

"No."

I sighed. "So much for Sherlock Karapoloff. This case is not going to be one of my successes."

Chris paused at the top of his sit-up. "No." And eased himself back down.

I frowned at him. "Do you know the meaning of the word *laconic*?"

He was on his way up. He might have smiled. "Yeah."

Bunky sat on the end of a black leather couch with the phone pressed to his ear. There was a smile in his voice but none on his face. "So you helped Phil carry Bonesaw in from the van after the party. Good for you, Daisy. You're a big girl, all right. Yes, the carrying case is heavy, isn't it. And where is Phil now?"

"And what about Cory?" I whispered. "He thinks he's going to hunt zombies. How does Bonesaw fit in? Is it a voodoo thing – snakes and zombies?"

Having finished his sit-ups, Chris stayed sitting up, his arms around his knees. He shook his head. "I don't know."

I was thinking about what Phil had planned for poor Cory. Bonesaw was a boa constrictor, so he wasn't poisonous. Was he going to . . . could he . . . *eat* Cory? I wondered. Surely not. And yet I remembered another Discovery Channel picture: a snake swallowing a goat.

Bunky was on his feet. "*What* did you say, Daisy?" His eyes behind his glasses were wide and staring. His charming phone manner – reminded me of someone, but I couldn't think who – was becoming strained. "I mean, are you sure, honey? And his friends too, eh? And did they say where they were going? Uh huh. Aren't you . . . smart to remember that." He checked his watch, swallowed. "Okay, thanks, Daisy. You're a real princess. No, I don't want to talk to your mom. You've told me all I need to know."

He closed the phone and gazed into space, chewing away on his lower lip like a dog worrying a week-old piece of garbage.

"Gone," he said.

"Phil?"

He nodded. "And his friends. Half an hour ago. And they've taken Bonesaw too."

CHAPTER 26 – *Start of the chase*

We all took a breath or two. I was arranging Bunky's news about Phil and company with the other facts in my mind, placing them side by side, seeing if I could make them fit together. Colin and Zach had taken Cory to the Aherne house by bus, where they had met Phil and Bonesaw, and now they were all gone to take part in some dreadful ritual that would scare the pants off Cory and give Phil his revenge. Mean of Phil, and ucky for Cory. I couldn't help remarking that Bonesaw was having a heck of an afternoon. First Jasmine's party, and now . . . well, I had a suspicion.

Miriam came back into the room with a crumpled-up wad of tissue in her hand. She looked grim.

"Bunky," she began. "Look what I found . . ."

The phone interrupted her. I could hear it ringing in the living room, kitchen, and somewhere upstairs.

Bunky held up a finger. "Hang on to that thought, babe. I think this may be my phone call."

Babe? I thought.

Did she like him? Is that why she'd changed clothes, got her hair mussed, and put on perfume? Is that why she let him call her babe?

She caught my eye for a second, and turned away. Her face and neck flooded with color.

Bunky took the phone call in the living room. Conversation was brief, and in Spanish – a language I don't know. Apart from *Buenas tardes, Señor E* and *Bogotá* and *Pearson Airport*, I didn't recognize any of the words. I could tell Bunky was upset, though. You don't have to know a language to know what's going on. I listen to my mom talking to my baba on the phone all the time. I could tell that Bunky was saying he was sorry, and that everything was okay, and that he'd do whatever it was he was supposed to have done – right away. Mom sounds like that when Baba is upset about something and she's trying to calm her down.

I wasn't thinking about Bunky's troubles. We had to find Cory. I had an idea. The pieces of the puzzle were fitting together in my mind. (Turned out I didn't have all the pieces. But I didn't know this at the time.)

Bunky slammed down the telephone receiver and ran through the hall, shaking his keys. "I'm off," he said, pushing his glasses up his sweaty nose. "If Señor E calls again, say I'm on my way to meet him."

"Are you going to Colombia?"

"No. He's here. He flew into Pearson this morning."

And he went through the door to the garage. We heard a car start with a roar and a squeal of rubber.

Miriam still held the tissue in her hand. "Oh, I never showed Bunky what I found in the pool filter. Do you think he'd want to see it, Chunky?"

I shrugged. I didn't know how I felt about her. When I thought about Bunky calling her babe, I was hurt. But when I looked into her eyes, and admired her syrup-blonde hair, and heard my pet name on her lips, I felt close to her.

My heart wasn't broken, but it seemed slightly bent. Love took on a different shape to fit it.

But whatever my heart said, the rest of me had a job to do. "Come on, Chris," I said. He was in the living room, punching buttons on the telephone. "We have to save Cory."

"Do you know where he is?"

"I think so," I said.

Chris and Miriam both wanted to know where we were going, and how we were getting there. So, feeling very much like the man, I told them my idea. Chris nodded. Miriam clapped her hands.

"Of course that's where they are," she said. "I should have thought of that. Good for you, Chunky."

Her certainty heartened me. "The name came up a couple of times. I even found it in the phone book."

"Jasmine's been there with her friends. I've heard her mention the place. And it won't take you long to get there on your raft. Fifteen minutes, half an hour maybe. The creek is a more direct route than the road. I wish I could come with you, but I have to stay with Valerie."

She didn't offer another kiss, and I didn't feel like taking one. Chris and I walked out the door in silence.

The sun was below the horizon. The air was still, retaining the heat of the day like a sponge.

"That last call came from the Prince Hotel," he told me. "Jasmine has call display and I saw the number."

"Makes sense." The Prince is a very expensive place not more than a ten-minute drive from where we were. "I guess that's where Señor E is staying."

We slid down the ravine in a cloud of dust. I gave my shorts a couple of perfunctory slaps, but Chris stopped to brush his clean.

"What if you're wrong, Jules?"

What if, indeed. "You think I'm wrong?"

He shook his head. "I think you're right. It's a good idea. But if we don't find Cory at the Rep House, what do we do then?"

"That police officer gave me her direct line," I said. "We'll call that."

And so began the last leg of our trip downstream. Considerably behind time, and minus a crew member, but we were going to get to the finish line – the M for museum (House, The Reptile) marked on the map.

We found the beached raft where we'd left it, with the pole and knapsack underneath, and shoved off. Chris's mouth was set tight.

"Don't like doing it this way," he told me.

"Without Cory, you mean?"

He nodded and pushed off.

The creek ran straight as an arrow for the first hundred yards, which was just as well because it took a while for our eyes to adjust to the evening light. The water was completely opaque – it was like gliding through asphalt. No way to avoid stumps or rocks because you couldn't see them.

We didn't talk much. Chris poled. I was thinking of all there was still to do. The things that had already gone wrong, and the things that might go wrong in the next half hour. What a mess.

Round the next bend, the creek widened and the banks dropped. The water moved steadily, eager to get to the lake. Chris stayed in the middle. Not far now.

On the right was a bluff, with lights from the houses on top. On the left was a gentler slope with a walking trail. We were in the gloaming, the purple-colored dusk lit with streamers of fire. The air was rich with the scents of earth and evergreen.

The birds were saying good-night. A particularly chatty pair kept at it for minutes on end. Sounded like they were saying, *See me hear you.* What liars – I could hear them fine. If I'd been able to see them, I might have told them to pipe down.

One more bend, left this time, and we were there. The bluff was behind us. We were surrounded by park-land: open spaces and small trees, a general air of grooming, tidiness. We passed a jogger, moving with fluid intent, earnest among the picnic benches. Ahead in the distance we could see the great emptiness that was the lake by night.

A minute later we came to a wooden bridge, wide enough for traffic. The creek was only a few feet below the road. There was a parking lot off to the left, and a great, gaunt dark shape off to the right.

This had to be the place.

Chris used the pole like a drag anchor, holding it against the stream bed to slow us down. I jumped off and pulled us toward the bank. Together, we tucked the raft neatly under the bridge, behind the pillar. You'd have to be looking for it to see it.

Time to go. But first . . .

I fished inside the knapsack and came up with the last juice box, and the last cookie. Ceremoniously, I split the cookie, gave half to Chris.

"For Cory," I whispered.

He nodded. "For Cory."

We ate the cookie, washed it down with the juice. I put the knapsack on top of the raft. Now it was time to go and rescue our friend.

It got an M on the map, but the Reptile House didn't look like much of a museum. With its sagging front porch, peeling paint, and broken upstairs windows, it looked more like a condemned hotel. We didn't go in, of course – not right away. First we walked carefully around the building, looking, listening. Chris led the way. He thought highly of my powers of persuasion, but this was his kind of thing.

I smelled clay, and lake water, and the end of a hot day. It was cooler than it had been an hour ago, and damper. I followed Chris's lithe athletic form around the perimeter of the old building, feeling like butterflies were barn dancing in my stomach.

By the front door was a billboard – REPTILE HOUSE – RENOVATION IN PROGRESS – but the only sign of renovation was a piece of rickety scaffolding that stood out like a skeleton, black against the twilit sky. In smaller letters at the bottom of the sign was: *Reptile House, Professor A. Aherne, Curator.*

Phil's dad. Of course. So much made sense.

Around the back was a staff parking lot. In the spot reserved for *Curator* was a dark minivan with a vanity license plate. REPDOC.

I felt the relief of a successful strategist – we were in the right place. But we still had the battle to fight. Was I ever nervous: my goose bumps had goose bumps. I had that being-watched feeling again too. When the dog barked, somewhere up on the hill, I bit my tongue.

I was wondering if we'd have to break in to the museum, but the front door swung open when Chris touched it. A bare hall led to a big open room. It was too dim to see details, but I could make out the outlines of large glass display cases.

He hissed gently, to get my attention, and pointed to the other side of the room, where a bar of light shone from under a door.

As we inched forward, I felt resistance piling up inside me. The closer we got to the door, the harder it was to move. The sign on it read, *Theater.* Now they hit me – big elephant-in-the-living-room doubts. I grabbed Chris's arm and pulled him down so that we were sitting on the floor behind one of the display cases.

"What are we doing here?" I whispered. "How can we rescue Cory? What are we thinking? Two of us are going to walk in and tell a gang of bigger kids to hand him over, and they will? I mean, they're older than us, and tougher than us, and way meaner than us. They set fire to that poor old Preacher guy. They can drive. They're practically grown-ups. And we're just kids. It's true, what Phil was saying, we have a clubhouse, with no girls allowed – no, you don't know what I'm talking about, you weren't there for that. Sorry. And on top of it all they have a scary snake. It's too much, man. We can't walk in and rescue Cory. We just can't do it. We're not good enough."

All this came spewing out like vomit, fast and uncontrollable, horrible to hear, horrible to go through. It left me weak and shaking, covered in sweat.

"Sorry, Chris." I turned my head away. Through the window I saw the evening sky. My first star came out. Also my second and third.

For a few breaths we sat there. When I turned back, I saw a glint of white. Chris was smiling.

"Done?" he said. "Feel better?"

"I don't know. I think so."

A few more breaths.

"I throw up before every basketball game," he said casually.

"No."

"Yep. Say I'm going to take a pee, but I go into a stall and heave, even if there's nothing in my stomach."

"But . . . you're such a good player."

Seems silly to say this, but it was a fixed point in my life, something to count on, like gravity. Chris *was* a good player.

"Yeah, how good? That's the point. Before every game there's the same fear. What if I screw up, miss a key shot, let them all down? Then they'll know."

"That . . . you're not as good as we think."

"Right."

I could feel the sweat cooling me as it dried on my skin. I tried to draw a parallel here.

"So you go out and play, even though you're scared, because not playing would be worse. Is that it?"

He nodded. Feet stretched out in front of us, backs to the display case, a couple of friends shooting the breeze. "I can't walk away from the team," he said. "I care about them. I care about what they think of me."

The team.

"You mean Cory." I'm not a sports guy. The team doesn't mean that much to me. But my friends do.

"Yeah. You care about Cory. And maybe me."

"Yeah, you too. You're right. Course you're right."

I thought about the worst thing that could happen here. We'd get beat up, laughed at, and whatever they could do with Bonesaw. That wouldn't be the worst thing. Walking away now, leaving Cory – that'd be worse.

"Sorry, Chris," I said for what seemed the dozenth time. I got to my feet. My brain was clear, my hands had stopped shaking. I felt . . . awful, actually. But better than before.

He got up too. "That's okay, I knew you weren't really going anywhere."

Headlights flashed across the window, highlighting the room for a second. The display cases loomed menacingly in the quick, shifting shadows.

What was a car doing down here? It began to circle the museum, disappearing around the side. It must be lost, I figured. It'd have to turn back in a moment. There was no road there.

I had to ask one more question. "Are you scared now?"

"Oh, yeah. But we have to save Cory."

"Because running away would be worse?"

"Because we said we would."

As nearly as I can figure the timing, the fire must already have started.

FIRE!

CHAPTER 27 – *Start of the big scene*

I felt this incredible sense of menace as I followed Chris to the theater door and put my ear to it. The reptiles would have been shipped away when the museum closed, but it was as if their spirits hung around. The room seemed filled with a thousand swords of Damocles.

"Do you smell something, Jules?" Chris whispered.

"Yes." Reptiles are stinky.

"Like something burning?"

I sniffed. "No, more like something rotting."

Through the door, I could hear rustling and murmuring, like mice behind the wall. The sounds were faint and far away. "Ready?" he whispered. I gave him the thumbs up. He opened the door and we slipped in like mist.

We were in a viewing gallery, maybe fifteen feet up, looking down. The stage had a leafy floor and a fake tree standing in the middle, reaching up almost as high as our gallery. Pretty cool, really. A room-sized terrarium.

The stage was lit and the gallery in deep shadow. We were invisible.

Two flattened boxes were lying end-to-end onstage. They looked like small plastic coffins. Phil, the gang leader, snake hook in hand, stood between them, talking.

"You must have got to Jasmine's party by the ravine door. I had Colin and Zach look for your raft. They found it, and you. They tricked you easily, Cory. They talked about a zombie ritual, and you left your friends and followed mine like a lamb. Didn't you?" He leaned over and rapped on the top of one of the cases with his hook. "Didn't you, Cory?"

I let out a deep breath. Beside me, Chris was nodding vehemently.

Found him.

After all we'd done this afternoon – after the bus rides, hitchhiking, forced labor, and rafting – it felt like finding Cory had become our second and more important quest for today. That part of the quest was now accomplished. Cory was found. He was onstage in the theater of the Reptile House Museum. In a carrying case.

"Are you scared in there, Cory? Sorry for laughing at me? I hope so. I hope you are so frightened you pee your pants. That's what I want. Once you've peed your pants, I'll let you go."

Laughter off to the side of the stage. Colin and Zach stood with their arms crossed.

I leaned over to speak next to Chris's ear. "What now?" I whispered.

He shook his head. "Wait and see."

Phil squatted between the cases. "Next door to you, Cory, is a grumpy boa named Bonesaw. He's from Colombia, and his name comes from the rounded pattern on his skin, which looks like the saw used to cut bone. I named him when my dad e-mailed me a picture of him, last year. My gang adopted the name. You said you didn't care about Bonesaw, Cory. Well, now's your chance to prove it."

He slid open the mesh panel door at the head of each carrying case and stood back. Now the two cases were open to each other. "Come on, Bonesaw!" he cried, poking his hook inside one of the cases. He was trying to get the snake to slither out of his own case and into Cory's.

"*No!*"

That was me. I climbed over the railing.

"No!"

I hung by my hands.

"No!"

I dropped onto the stage.

Sometimes it's easy. Sometimes you know what to do, and all the fears and doubts vanish like smoke in the wind. There was no way – NO WAY – that this was going to happen. My friend trapped in a coffin case with a boa constrictor crawling in to visit? No way. I didn't care that Phil had a hook, or that he and his friends were all older, larger, tougher than me.

"I'm here, Cory!" I shouted.

To answer your question, I did not feel courage descending onto my shoulders like a mantle. Climbing down from the gallery was bad. But staying up there was worse. I could not watch while they bullied Cory. It was *easier* to get involved, even if it meant getting beaten up. I bet it would be easier to be tortured than to watch it (though I sincerely hope I never have to prove that one).

My arrival put Phil right off his stride. "How –" he started.

"How did I get here? Wouldn't you like to know, Phil. But I'm not alone. This place is surrounded." I kept talking, hoping I'd say something useful. "Your revenge idea is finished, Phil. And you and your friends are in trouble."

I ran to the two cases and pulled them apart. Bonesaw seized his opportunity to escape. You've been hearing about Bonesaw for ages now, but this is your first sight of him, so let me take a second to describe him. He poured out of his case and onto the floor in a clean, dark line that kept on coming. I thought he'd never end. Whoa! A big boy indeed. He was moving too fast for me to pick out any saw-shaped designs on his skin. All I got was that he was brownish and blotchy. And thick! His head was as big as my outstretched hand and his middle was way bigger around than my thigh. Could he swallow a goat? A Cory? Maybe not, but I'd hate to be a cat or a dog or a baked ham sitting near him when he was hungry.

He wrapped himself around the fake dead tree and started climbing. I dropped to my knees and reached into Cory's case, grabbing a handful of hair. *That* threw me for a second. I couldn't think of Cory without his red cap. Then I started pulling.

You'd think Phil would have worried about the snake, but he didn't. He swung his hook and hit me in the back. Ow! The hook wasn't sharp, so it didn't stick into me. But it still hurt – like being hit with a golf club. He would have hit me again, only Chris launched himself from the gallery, landing on his shoulders. The two of them went down together. Zach and Colin charged in to rescue their leader.

Cory tried to wriggle out of the case, but he got stuck at the shoulders. They must have had a heck of a time cramming him in. He lay on the ground, looking like a mythical creature: a box with the head of a man. The Greeks would have a word for him.

Zach tried to pick me up. (Ha ha, very funny. No, I didn't mean it like that. I'm not that kind of guy.) What I mean is he grabbed my shoulder and leg and tried to dead-lift me like a barbell. What an idiot. A barbell stays still. I didn't. He got me up to about head height and then had to drop me. Ha ha on him. No, wait. I was the one falling, landing with the point of my hip on Cory's box.

Ha ha on me.

Good news, though. I smashed the box with my fall, and Cory pulled himself free. He got slowly to his feet, groggy after all that time lying down.

Colin knocked him to the floor.

Something fell on my head. A stone or something. I ignored it, helping Cory stand up again. Not for long. Phil bounced into him by accident and knocked him down. Zach put his arms around me (no, no, still not like that. I tell you, I'm not interested) and threw me to the ground. Phil jumped on me on purpose.

Yes, it was an old-fashioned fight. Good guys and bad guys. Rafters and Bonesaws. We had right and justice on our side, but so what? They were stronger. Colin was knocking Cory down faster than he could get up. Phil held his hook across my chest, pinning me to the floor. Zach had Chris pushed against the wall. (When I saw the two guys face to face, their similarity was clearer than ever. Both had the same wide-set eyes, high cheek-bones, firm chins. Really, you forgot that one was white and one black.)

Another stone or something hit my head. What was going on? Bits of the ceiling falling? I looked up, and there was Bonesaw, directly over my head. He was twisted around the top of the tree like a pretzel, with his tail drooping toward me. It quivered, and . . . here came a third stone. Wait a minute! I picked it out of my hair, warm, sticky, and smelling of . . .

"Yeck!" I cried at the top of my lungs, startling everyone into a momentary hush. "Bonesaw is pooping on me!"

CHAPTER 28 – *What's really going on*

The hush fell like a glass bowl onto a concrete floor – one minute whole and perfect, the next shattered into a million pieces.

Everyone laughed. Phil rolled off me, his mouth opened wide, showing his crazed serrations. Zach, who had been going to punch Chris, whirled round so quickly that he fell over, and everyone laughed some more. I thought Cory and Colin were both going to have heart attacks.

I guess it was pretty funny. Poop can make boys laugh any time, and someone getting pooped on from above is hard to beat.

I glared around the room – at my friends and enemies, at Bonesaw overhead, at Bunky crouched by the empty carrying case.

Wait a minute. *Bunky?* "When did you get here?" I cried.

He straightened up but didn't give me a straight answer. "I came as soon as my meeting was over."

"How did you know to come to the museum?"

"Daisy told me where her brother was headed." He glared at Phil, who stuck out his tongue. That one exchange gave away their relationship, I thought. Bunky was older, but he worked for Phil's dad. He couldn't control Phil, and they both knew it.

"Show me the snake poop, Jules."

Of course we laughed. Poop.

"Shut up! All of you, shut up!" Bunky was under a strain. He did not sound like the charming smooth operator he'd been an hour earlier.

"Does your snake poop look like this?" he asked me, holding out his hand. In it was a piece of green rock about the size of a Timbit and the texture of a smoker's lung.

I pointed to the three offerings, which had all landed on the floor near the base of the fake tree. Bunky bent to pick them up.

Phil laughed. "Look at the guy who collects snake poop."

"Shut up, Phil. You've already done more harm than you know." Bunky put the samples in a sealable plastic bag. "I found these stones in Bonesaw's carrying case. What *did* you think you were doing, moving him around after I told you not to?"

Stones, I thought. What did he mean, stones?

"*You* shut up," said Phil. "You can't boss me around."

"Ow!" Zach was staring at his hand. "That wall is *hot*. And look at the smoke!"

He pointed at an outlet, from which a thin stream of gray rose in a lazy trickle.

We all moved away from the hot wall. I looked round for an EXIT sign – the first time in my life when one of those would have come in handy. I didn't see one, but I did notice an open door at the back of the stage. Bunky must have come through it.

No silence is absolute. Silence is the small sounds you hear when no one is shouting. In this silence I could hear faint but definite movement from behind the wall – small crackling noises. Reminded me of the time we found carpenter ants in our bathroom door. Put your ear to it and you heard them in there, chewing away. Brr.

A voice spoke from the viewing gallery, in the heart of the darkness overhead.

"I'll take the stones."

I only ever heard this voice say a few phrases, but it is with me still. How to give you a sense of its power? It was a voice like a V-8 engine, throttled back and throaty. And so deep. *So* deep. Think Darth Vader with a head cold. He didn't speak loudly, but his voice filled the room. I could practically feel it through the floor.

Bunky jumped when he heard it. "Oh, uh, hi, Señor E," he said, shielding his eyes to peer up. "I thought you were going to stay in the car."

"I wanted to see why my investment was taking so long to collect." Señor E spoke careful English, with a whisper of accent.

"I explained back in Bogotá," said Bunky. "Boas are delicate creatures, and sometimes they get . . . well . . . constipated."

No one giggled at constipated, which was strange. I think we were all in awe of the voice. Not even Phil made a joke.

Bunky smiled nervously. Held up the plastic bag. "Here you go. The G-I tract is doing its thing at last. Direct service from Colombia to Scarborough."

"Where is the fifth stone?"

Señor E leaned forward, bringing his face into the light from the stage. A long, wrinkled face, with a sharp nose like the front of a sailing ship. I'd never seen it before, but you have, if you read that piece of preface at the very beginning. Or did you read it and forget?

"The fifth stone is still . . . inside, I guess," said Bunky.

"Give me what you have."

Bunky stepped forward and tossed the bag lightly into the gallery. I heard a clinking sound as Señor E caught it.

"Ha ha!" said Cory. "He wants a bag of poop!" He turned to Zach, standing next to him. "Do you believe it? That guy up there wants a bag of poop."

"Not poop, Cory. Stones." Thoughts spilled into my head like light into a darkened room, revealing objects I hadn't known were there. "Dark green stones from Colombia, carried in the body of a large snake. These guys," I said, "are smuggling emeralds."

The hot wall dissolved into flames. It took about three seconds from the time the first flickering finger poked through the electrical outlet to the entire wall looking like a sheet of fire. Scariest thing I saw that day. Scariest thing I have ever seen.

I jumped back. And a whole lot of things happened real quick.

CHAPTER 29 – Beginning of the end

"Jules! Are you asleep?"

My mom's voice. It's after my bedtime and she can see that my light's on.

"Just doing a bit of writing."

It's so comfortable writing in bed. You can lie back and think of your next sentence. If you get stuck, you can fall asleep. I got the idea of working here from a book about ancient Greece. Those old guys ate in bed too. What a life. No wonder they invented philosophy.

"Well, don't stay up too late."

"Okay. Good-night."

"Good-night, little Jules. Mommy loves you."

Got to hurry along. Chris gets back from the cottage tomorrow, in time for my birthday. He's going to call me the minute he lands. I want to be able to show him the whole story, right up to the The End. If it seems like I'm rushing this last part, well, I am.

Here's the way I remember it: Bunky threw the bag of jewels to Señor E in the gallery, I made my brilliant deduction about emerald smuggling, and the wall burst into flame. Then Bonesaw dropped from the fake tree onto Bunky's head, knocking him to the floor and streaking out the door in the back wall. Bunky, dazed from the fall, lurched after the snake with his arms outstretched, calling the snake's name. At least that's what I figure he was calling. It came out, "Bones! . . . Bones!"

Cory stared. "Is he a zombie?" he asked. "Or just acting like one?"

Snake and herpetologist (that right? I can't be bothered getting out of bed to check. I spent hours on the Internet today, researching about snakes) vanished out the door, leaving the theater to us kids, and Señor E in the gallery.

He smiled down at us, his face clearly visible in the light from the inferno. His tongue flicked out to lick his lips. The wall of flame was creeping toward him, but he didn't seem worried. In fact, he seemed quite at home surrounded by fire.

"Help!" I called.

He shook his head, still smiling. "You know too much," he said.

"But you can't just leave us here to die! Phone the fire department! We don't have much time! We're trapped."

Señor E laughed, a genuine expression of merriment. "Trapped in flames," he said. He really thought this was funny. His mirth filled the room the way an organ fanfare fills a church, the way a fart fills a sleeping bag. Cory stared up at him, his eyes bulging like plums. Señor E left the gallery, but his laughter lingered for a moment before being swallowed in the roar of the fire.

We got out of there in a hurry.

Easy decision in the corridor behind the theater. To our right: a burning restaurant. (*Great lunch spot*, they said down by the river. *But don't order the lamb.*) To our left: a metal staircase going up. We climbed, our feet crashing like cymbals. The staircase led up to a storeroom with a ladder built into the brick wall. We climbed some more and found ourselves on the roof.

"So, your name is Jules," said the detective, "and you were the one who discovered that they were smuggling jewels. Funny, huh? Jewels and Jules."

We were sitting in an interview room at 41 Division, the police station on Elgin Avenue at Birchmount. Just me and Detective Strongman. It was almost midnight, and I was as tired as . . . something really tired. Too tired to think about exactly how tired I was.

"Yeah. A riot." I took a drink from a water bottle. They'd offered me juice, but I'd been drinking juice all day.

"How long have you known Bunky?"

"I met him today for the first time. I'd never met any of these guys before today. Not Bunky, or Phil, or Señor E, or the guys from the gang, or Miriam. I said all this already. It's on the film there."

I pointed to the blackened window – there was a camera behind it.

"I know, son. That's how we do things." The detective was a kindly guy with a big jaw, a brush cut, and a rumpled blue suit. If you are what you eat, he was a big piece of prime rib. He held up the clear evidence bag. In it was the uncut emerald that Miriam had found trapped in the pool filter. This was Señor E's fifth stone, though the first one, uh, *processed* by Bonesaw. The myrtle-colored chunk of Colombia (Cory had spent thirty seconds trying to come up with the exact shade of greeny-gray) was longer than my thumb. It had to be ten times bigger than any jewel I had ever seen in a ring or necklace.

"Think of this being worth as much as my house," the detective said, shaking his head. "Now, Jules, I want to know more about the fire."

A knock on the door, and Walter stuck his head in the room. He looked tougher in uniform, as if the blue fabric was a kind of double-sided armor, protecting him from the world outside and his own feelings inside. Hard to imagine him crying for a dead friend. "Sorry to interrupt, detective, but the boys' parents have arrived." He gave me a cop smile. "Your mom hasn't stopped talking yet, Jules."

"Thanks, Walter," said the detective. "Put them in my office. I'll see them now. Anything else?"

Walter looked at his clipboard. "The Feds are on their way to take over the smuggling case, but their car broke down. They don't want you talking to anyone about jewels until they get here. The Aherne boy, Philip, and his two friends are lawyered up. They want to be helpful because they are due to travel to Africa in a week. The parents of the girl, Miriam, want to take her home. That vagrant Ernesto is just about finished his statement, and his third sandwich. I think that's it, sir. Oh, and we've had our first call from the media."

"What about?"

"Runaway boa constrictor."

"Runaway – oh crap!"

Crap indeed. Maybe I'm going too fast here. You must be wondering how we got down from the burning building, and where all the people came in – Miriam and Ernesto and the cops. Fair enough. Let me back up.

CHAPTER 30 – *Middle of the end*

S o we found ourselves on the flat top of the roof at the Reptile House, Chris, Cory and me, Phil and the gang, and Bunky. There was a waist-high iron railing around the flat part, and steep sides – like the Addams Family place. The fire was on the side of the museum facing away from the parking lot. Smoke curled and billowed, and I could see the glow on that side when I looked down.

Bunky had his phone out. His face twitched like a bad satellite picture on TV. "And there's a snake missing!" He pressed his free hand to his free ear. He still looked stunned. "Hello? Hello? Are you there? Can anyone hear me?"

"Where'd Bonesaw go?" Chris asked.

Phil pointed down to the parking lot. "Slithered off the roof that-a-way," he said. "Must have fallen to the ground. We didn't want to try to stop it."

"How come?" said Cory. "Scared of the little snakey?"

Being kidnapped, terrorized, and locked in a snake case hadn't changed Cory at all. His personality was like a non-stick frying pan – it cleaned really easily. I was going to tell him to shut up, but I thought, No. He'd earned the right to insult Phil.

Bunky closed the phone. "Anyone hear a fire engine?" he asked.

I heard the hissing of the fire, and the creak of the roof beams as we shifted around. I heard a dog barking in the distance. But no sirens. I wondered if Bunky had, in fact, got through to the emergency people. And when I say I *wondered*, I mean I was really concerned.

But I can't wonder about one thing for long – my brain gets distracted. I thought about the fire, and then the snake escaping the fire, and then the stones inside the snake.

Emeralds were the last piece in the jigsaw puzzle. Like boa constrictors, they come from Colombia. Bunky was the link. He was down there studying snakes with Professor Aherne, but his dad was a jewel tycoon. Bunky would know what boas eat. He'd know that if you put an emerald inside a dead rat, say, and fed it to a snake, you had a perfect way to get stones across the border. Using the snake to mule product. I remembered his concern for how many days Bonesaw had gone without pooping. It was a pretty good plan – almost funny too.

The fire smell reminded me of the campfire we were supposed to be having at the end of our raft trip. I thought about s'mores, chocolate melting on the graham crackers, with the baby marshmallows standing out like jewels. Which brought me back.

"How much are the jewels worth?" I asked Bunky.

"Still one left," he said. "Got to find the snake. Raw, uncut Muzo emeralds – exceptional quality – hundred and nineteen carats."

He rocked back and forth, the phone at his ear. The dog kept barking, in a rhythmic pattern. *Yap yap yap.*

Pause. *Yap yap yap.* The sound was coming from near the bridge. I had to wonder if the old lady was planning to walk her dog to the little museum to chase sticks and dig. Not tonight, Satan.

Seconds passed like one of Dad's kidney stones.

The flames curled over the steep part of the roof. They looked like waves, with sparks of foam blowing off them into the night. The fire was past the corner now, established on two sides of the building. And still no sirens.

In movies, when the band of heroes realizes they are doomed, they act bravely and movingly. Firm jaws, ironic smiles, maybe a single manly tear. Not much of that here. Bunky kept calling 9-1-1 to ask when they were coming. He must have called ten times. Phil and Zach were taking turns slapping Colin, who was whimpering. Cory was in some strange Cory place, mesmerized by the fire. I couldn't tell if this was a nightmare for him or some pyromaniac dream come true.

Chris fit the movie. He gave me a tight half smile.

I wonder if he felt like throwing up? I didn't. This situation did not terrify me the way the tornado had terrified me, or the plunge in deep water where I'd lost my glasses. I was not upset, as I had been in the dark outside the theater door a half hour ago. I was calm, removed from feeling. I went outside myself, trying to see my predicament from someone else's point of view. I floated down to the parking lot and stared up at the kids on top of the burning museum. How will they get down?

I asked myself. *And I came up with an answer.* So inevitable did this answer seem, in my daydream, that when a familiar small, dirty, tousled head popped over the edge of the roof, I was hardly surprised at all.

"Ernesto," I said.

"Ah, Jewel!" he said. "And Captain Marvel."

"You're on the scaffolding, aren't you, Ernesto?" In my mind's eye I saw the metal tubing against the outer wall of the museum.

He smiled. "The scaffolding does not quite reach to the roof. Right now I am standing on Maid Marian's shoulders."

He found a handhold in the slates of the steep roof, transferred his weight, and drew one leg up carefully onto the eavestrough. Then the other. "Pass up the rope," he called, and Miriam's hand appeared, holding a coil of yellow nylon rope.

"Hi, Miriam!" I called.

"Hi, Chunky!"

We were all crowding around this side of the roof. Ernesto was directly below us, balanced like the acrobat he used to be.

"That looks like my rope!" called Chris.

"It is your rope." Ernesto gathered arm's lengths of it. "We found it in your knapsack. Now, catch!"

He threw, almost overbalancing. Chris caught the rope. He didn't need to be told what to do. In three or four well-coordinated motions, he looped it around the railing and made it fast. "Clove hitch," he said.

"Gesundheit," I said.

He grinned and snapped the yellow nylon, sending a ripple down to the roof edge.

"Pay attention, everyone," he announced, "while I demonstrate a mountaineering technique known as . . . rappelling."

Rappelling. Oh, right. Jumping off a cliff holding on to a rope.

"You and your *Survival Handbook*," I said.

One by one we made our way down the rope to the edge of the roof. Ernesto and Miriam helped us onto the scaffolding, and we climbed down to the ground. Chris went first, to show us how. Bunky went next because he was the scaredest. When he tried to talk to Miriam, she got angry and told him to shut up.

My heart sang.

Only one of us at a time on the scaffolding. It was seriously rickety. Bunky shrieked on the way down. Miriam told him to shut up again.

Colin recognized Ernesto. "Hey, short stuff!" he said. "I remember chasing you. That was fun."

Ernesto's face was a careful blank. When Colin was feeling his way toward the scaffolding, Ernesto kicked him in the side of the knee. Colin screamed and almost fell, grabbing on to the eavestrough just in time.

"Now *that* was fun," said Ernesto.

Zach and Phil went carefully. Cory slid down the roof, shouting, "Whee!" and barely using the rope. The fire was moving across this side of the building by then.

My turn came last. Ernesto had a huge smile for me. Miriam squeezed my hand hard. She'd changed back into shorts and was carrying the empty knapsack on her back. She explained about meeting Ernesto down by the creek. She'd been on her rope swing. He'd been walking. Miriam wanted to help us rescue Cory but didn't know how to get through the woods in the dark. Ernesto knew the path night or day, rain or shine. He recognized our names when she told him and said he would be happy to guide her.

"He seemed to think he owed you a favor," she said.

As Miriam and I climbed down, we heard the sirens. The fire department had come just after the nick of time. They roared down the hill and around the bend, two of Scarborough's finest, with cop cars behind them. The lead truck swerved wildly near the bridge. There was an ominous crunching sound and a hiss of air brakes that I could hear all the way across the parking lot. The truck ended up jammed sideways against the bridge. Two cop cars parked on the edge of the creek bank.

The scaffolding fell over.

That's right. There was a low groan as the metal supports gave out, and the whole structure folded slowly sideways, like a lawn chair. I guess it could have gone at any time. Miriam and I jumped easily onto the grass. We were so near the ground, we didn't even stumble. The scaffolding collapsed behind us with a muffled clanking sound, like a knight in armor falling into a feather bed.

I waved up at Ernesto, who waved shakily back. He stood on the eavestrough with the end of the rope in his hands. The fire was directly below him – he couldn't use the rope to rappel down.

Firefighters were running up now, pushing us away from the building, yelling questions. *Were we okay? Was anyone still inside?* Big, heavy guys in uniforms, sounding calm and mad as hell at the same time.

"There's someone on the roof!" I called. "Bring the ladder!"

A tall firefighter with a thin, drawn face and a beaked nose, like an eagle, looked up, shading his eyes against the glare of the flames.

He swore quietly. "We can't bring a ladder, kid. Our driver swerved because he . . . well, he *thought* he saw something slithering across his path. Truck is jammed against the bridge abutment. We can't move it until we get a crane."

He swore again.

Miriam grabbed my arm. "We can't let Ernesto die up there, Jules. Think of something!"

And I did. I had the picture all at once, in living color, just the way Ernesto had told it to me.

"Do you have a net?" I asked the firefighter, who stopped muttering about stupid rookie drivers who thought Scarborough was the Amazon rainforest.

"A life net? Yeah, there's one stowed in the ladder truck somewhere. Do you really think that old guy up there would jump?"

"That old guy is a retired human cannonball."

The beaky firefighter gaped, then started talking quickly into his headset. Thirty seconds later the life net was ready, a giant parachute with eight uniforms stretching it tight. Four kids – three rafters and Miriam – cheered from a safe distance. (Three other kids – known gang members – were being questioned by police about how the fire started.)

Ernesto dived from the heart of the smoke and flame. He managed a somersault on the way down.

After hearing our stories, the police decided to take us all to the station to answer questions and make statements. I guess it was hard to believe, let alone make sense of. "A boa constrictor?" the officer who was questioning us three kept saying. "You boys sure you mean a boa constrictor?" Yes, we said.

A young firefighter with freckles overheard us. "Hear that, Captain?" he said. "There is a snake out there. I knew I saw something."

"Shut it, rookie," growled the beaky firefighter. "You still screwed up."

Bunky tried to run away, which was stupid because they caught him almost at once and put him in handcuffs. He went in the first car, along with Ernesto and Miriam. The Bonesaw gang went in the second car.

The station was sending another car for Chris, Cory, and me. We walked to the parking lot to wait for it. With the bridge blocked, we had to splash across the creek. The raft was still parked under the bridge. Chris and I noticed it at the same time and showed Cory. "Oh, yeah," he said. A simple thing, a collection of logs cut from fallen poplars, lashed together at both ends to make a platform big enough to support three boys. That raft had taken us a long way – much farther than the map would show. We stopped for a moment.

"Let's let the raft go," I said.

They knew what I meant right away. We hustled it out from under the bridge and into the middle of the stream. I stood at the bow, Chris and Cory on either side. The water pulled gently on my calves.

"Ready?"

They nodded. I splashed out of the way and let the raft drift. We climbed up on the bank and followed its course downstream. The creek ran straight and deep. The raft got hung up only once, and not for long. In less than a minute it hit the lake. A young moon rose in the south, making a silver pathway across the calm dark water. The raft stayed in view, drifting farther and farther from shore.

"Good-bye," I said softly.

"You talking to the raft?" said Chris.

"Not really," I said.

"Didn't think so."

"Know what I feel like eating?" said Cory. "Gelato. That's what."

I had the knapsack slung over one shoulder. Miriam had given it to me, along with a peck on the cheek.

"All we have left to eat is ketchup packets," I said.

I saw a shadow move behind the front bumper of a fire truck. I remembered the barking dog. "Satan?" I whispered. "Is that you?"

The shadow moved – not a dog. It was making for the stream.

"Bonesaw!"

The snake moved awkwardly, heavily over the stones. I thought I knew why. Of course he'd be hungry after all the excitement. "What did you catch, Bonesaw?"

No answer, except a plop and a ripple from under the bridge.

CHAPTER 31 – *The end*

I hate epilogues too, so I won't be long here. I don't have much left to say anyway. I told Detective Strongman all I knew about the fire. The next day I went downtown and told a different detective all I knew about the jewels. Since then I've been busy writing. It's getting on for one in the morning, and I'm tired, so I'll wrap it up fast.

First, what I haven't done. I haven't seen Ernesto again. I never did find out how his life fell apart. I guess I never will. You can't know all the stories. I haven't seen Roscoe either. Or Marty and Vince. I don't know what Phil or Bernadette or Jasmine are up to. They may still be in Africa, for all I know. I keep meaning to go to Elgin Avenue for the bike drop, but I haven't got around to it yet.

I did see Zach the other day. He must have learned something about himself, because he was volunteering at a homeless shelter. Ha ha, just kidding. He was on a subway platform, going the opposite way from me. He shot me with his finger.

I don't always take the subway. I've had a few rides in the car Miriam bought with her reward money. No one could figure out who the uncut emerald belonged to, so the organized crime unit hung onto it and gave her a percentage of its value. Miriam can't drive by herself yet, so

I get to ride with her and her mom. Yes, Jules and two ladies. It's weird – but interesting.

(Funny thing about Miriam. Last time we were chatting online, some guy named *hunkaburninglove* signed on and gave her directions to his place. What's that about?)

Yes, I said organized crime, because that's what Señor E is. Cory drew a caricature of him, which I thought was brilliant considering he'd only seen him in firelight for a second. The cops liked the caricature enough to fax it to Bogotá, and the cops there recognized him. His real name is Enrique, and he's high up in the Colombian mob. He and his four emeralds have disappeared, but Cory is getting a police commendation.

Bunky and his lawyers are still talking to the cops. He's been charged with a bunch of things including smuggling and cruelty to animals.

Professor Aherne flew home to issue a statement, then flew back to the jungle somewhere. There are no plans to rebuild the museum.

Speaking of which, investigators concluded that the fire was not the result of arson. They found some underground live wiring that had been dug up and chewed – but whether the chewing was done by a rat or a dog or some other digging animal, they couldn't tell.

Oh, yeah, I had my birthday party. The big one-four. Guess what Baba got me? I'll give you a hint – it's got polka dots. Mom is saying I should write her a thank-you note.

All right, two more stories and I'm done.

I had to go to the bathroom at the police station. While I was sitting there, I heard a deep, resonant voice ask, "Have you finished?"

I panicked. "No, no!" I called out. "I'm not done yet. Don't flush."

Silence.

"Because if you've finished, Bill," said the deep voice, "I'd like to use the sink."

"Sure, sarge," said another voice. "I'm finished. Help yourself." I heard the towel dispenser, and then footsteps heading out the bathroom door.

I do not see how talking toilets can ever catch on.

I just woke up from a dream I've been having the last couple nights or so. Cory, Chris, and I are climbing up a steep mountain road. The mountain itself dominates the skyline above us. We're getting close to the top, and we turn to look back. Wow, I think. Haven't we come a long way! Look at all the signposts we've passed. Away in the distance, at the base of the mountain, I can just make out the green field where our journey started.

We turn back to our task, and struggle up the last few gasping steps to the summit – only to find that the great height we've conquered is *not* the mountain at all, but a foothill. Having got this far, to this small summit, we can now see how much higher we still have to climb.

The mountain soars above us, impossibly vast.

ACKNOWLEDGMENTS

S ome books come out better than you think they're going to. *Into The Ravine* is one of them. I didn't work any harder than usual on it, but the end result makes it look like I did. Lots of people to thank here. Publisher Kathy Lowinger asked for some fireside stories and didn't blench at all when I turned in a suburban Huck Finn instead. Agent Scott Treimel's unsolicited compliments on the first draft were surprising (he usually hates my stuff) and heartening. Designer Jennifer Lum's cover was a revelation – when I saw the rough I nearly did a spit-take with my coffee. Copy editor Heather Sangster provided the finishing touches. Thank you all. On a technical note, the raft-building, rappelling, and general nature lore are borrowed from Peter Darman's *The Survival Handbook* (London: Amber Books, 1994). If you are planning your own river trip, please (please!) follow his excellent advice rather than mine and Jules's. Sergeant Darren S. of the Port Hope Police Department willingly shared his knowledge of police procedure, but I couldn't hear him very well because the bar was crowded. My baba had a powerful voice; I'm glad to have had my mom's help in rendering her Macedonian and Macedonian-English phrases. And a final thank you to my kids for providing me with names and stories, for confirming usage when I was in doubt, and in general for laughing at my jokes and putting up with me.